Seventeen Wishes

ROBIN JONES GUNN

BETHANY HOUSE PUBLISHERS
MINNEAPOLIS, MINNESOTA 55438

Seventeen Wishes
Revised edition 1999
Copyright © 1993, 1999
Robin Jones Gunn

Edited by Janet Kobobel Grant
Cover illustration and design by Lookout Design Group, Inc.

This story is a work of fiction. All characters and events are the product of the author's imagination. Any resemblance to any person, living or dead, is coincidental. Text has been revised and updated by the author.

Focus on the Family books are available at special quantity discounts when purchased in bulk by corporations, organizations, churches, or groups. Special imprints, messages, and excerpts can be produced to meet your needs. For more information, contact: Resource Sales Group, Focus on the Family, 8605 Explorer Drive, Colorado Springs, CO 80920; or phone (800) 932-9123.

A Focus on the Family book published by
Bethany House Publishers
A Ministry of Bethany Fellowship International
11400 Hampshire Avenue South
Bloomington, Minnesota 55438
www.bethanyhouse.com

Printed in the United States of America by
Bethany Press International, Bloomington, Minnesota 55438

Library of Congress Cataloging-in-Publication Data

Gunn, Robin Jones, 1955–
    Seventeen Wishes / Robin Jones Gunn
        p. cm. — (The Christy Miller Series ; 9)
    Summary: Sixteen-year-old Christy goes to summer camp determined to pack her time with romantic memories.
    ISBN 1–56179–730–8
    [1. Camps—Fiction. 2. Christian life—Fiction.] I. Title.
II. Title: Seventeen wishes. III. Series: Gunn, Robin Jones, 1955–
Christy Miller Series ; 9.
PZ7.G972Se   1993
[Fic]—dc20   93–11278
                                                CIP
                                               AC

---

02 03 04 05 06 07 08 09 / 18 17 16 15 14 13 12 11 10 9 8 7 6

Contents

CHAPTER ONE

Act Natural

"Are you sure you told the guys we were coming this afternoon?" red-headed Katie Weldon asked her best friend, Christy Miller, as they ascended the outdoor steps of the apartment building.

"Of course. I told Todd yesterday we would leave right after church. He said it would take about an hour to drive down here," Christy answered, her long legs taking the stairs two at a time. "The directions were really clear. I'm sure this is the place."

"Number twelve is at the end there," Katie pointed out. Then striking her usual athletic stance, she knocked on the door. No one answered. Katie looked into Christy's distinctive blue-green eyes with an unspoken, "Well? What do we do now?"

Christy bit her lower lip and scanned the piece of paper in her hand. "I know this is right. Knock again. Louder."

Katie pounded her fist on the door and called out, "Hey, Rick, Doug, Todd. We're here!"

Still no answer.

Christy brushed her nutmeg brown hair off her forehead and cautiously peered in a window. From what she could see, no one was inside. "What should we do, Katie?"

"They're probably playing a joke on us. They know what a big deal it was for you to talk your parents into letting you come to San Diego. They're probably trying to freak us out. You know, the 'big college guys teasing the little high school girls' trick."

Katie sounded so confident of her answer that Christy almost believed her. But then Katie usually sounded confident.

"Should we find a phone and try to call them?" Christy suggested.

"Lower your voice," Katie warned. "If they're in there, they can hear what you're saying."

"I don't think they're here. Maybe they ran to the store or something," Christy said, looking around.

Below them she noticed a cement courtyard with a swimming pool surrounded by lounge chairs. "Why don't we go down by the pool and wait for them?"

Katie surveyed the situation, her bright green eyes scanning the apartment complex for any sign of life. "Doesn't it seem weird to you," she whispered, "that for a place that's supposed to be crawling with college students, nobody's around?"

Christy was starting to get the heebie-jeebies. "Come on. Let's go down by the pool. At least we won't look so obviously lost, standing by their door with our luggage."

"Oh yeah, we'll look real natural lounging around the pool wearing jeans and clutching our luggage. If anyone from these other apartments sees us, they'll probably think we're homeless and call the police," Katie sputtered as she followed Christy down the stairs to the pool.

"Then let's put our stuff back in the car."

"Good idea. I'm starting to feel like an orphan. Why would they ditch us like this? You would think one of them could manage to leave a note or something."

The two girls stood at the trunk of Katie's car while she fished for her keys. "Did I give you my keys?"

"Very funny," Christy said. "Of course I don't have your keys. Stop goofing around and open the trunk."

"I can't find them."

Christy let out a sigh. "Did you leave them in the car?"

They both peered in the front window and at the same time noticed the keys dangling from the ignition. Of course, all the doors were locked.

"Good, Katie. Real swift! Now what are we supposed to do?" Christy snapped.

"Hey, relax, will you? I've done this before. All I need is a coat hanger."

"And where are we supposed to find a coat hanger?"

"Let's try the dumpster over there," Katie suggested.

She opened the gates to the garbage area and began to rummage through trash bags.

Christy stood nervously beside the car, guarding their gear. Now they really looked like a couple of bums with Katie sifting through the trash.

This was supposed to be a nice, simple, Memorial weekend in San Diego to visit the guys' God-Lovers Bible study and to have a fun trip to the zoo. It's turning into a disaster!

"Found one!" Katie called out, lifting her prized coat hanger into the air. A rotten banana peel clung to her arm.

"Nice work," Christy said. "Now why don't you try to leave the rest of the garbage in the dumpster?"

Katie beamed a victory smile as she shook off the banana peel and straightened out the hanger. She cheerfully gave Christy a rundown of the last time she had locked her keys in the car.

"I was at work, and I had to go in the mall to find a clothing store that would give me a hanger. I figured out that time how to make the loop on the end just right so it'll catch on the knob there. Good thing my car is so old. Your car doesn't have locks like this. We'd be stuck if it were your car."

Christy kept glancing around, aware that now they looked like homeless, garbage-digging hoboes and car thieves.

"Can you hurry it up, Katie?"

"I almost have it," she said, gingerly wedging the hanger between the window and door frame and maneuvering the loop over the lock button. Her tongue stuck out slightly, and she squinted her eyes.

Christy thought Katie looked as if she were playing one of those games at the video arcade in which the player has to manipulate a metal claw inside a glass cage to pick up a small stuffed animal. Christy could never win that game. She had ceased wasting her quarters on it long ago.

Not Katie. Katie was always up for a challenge. Anytime, anywhere.

"Almost," Katie breathed between clenched teeth as the two girls pressed their faces against the car window, pleading with the loop to connect with the black peg.

"Hey!" a loud voice called out behind them.

They jumped and spun around. They were surprised to see that the big voice belonged to a petite Asian girl.

"Are you Todd's friends?" she asked.

She had a bag of groceries in her arms and apparently had arrived on foot, which explained why they hadn't heard her approach. Her long, silky black hair hung over her shoulders, and she peered at them with a delicate smile.

"Yes!" Christy said eagerly. Then feeling obligated to explain what they were doing, she quickly added, "We locked the keys in the car, and we're trying to get them out."

Katie continued recounting their adventure. "We went to the guys' apartment, but no one was there. We thought maybe they were playing a trick on us, which would be typical of those guys, but they never jumped out and said 'Boo,' so we thought we would put our stuff back in the car."

The girl listened as they rattled on with their nervous explanations.

"That's when we found out the keys were locked in the car," Christy said.

Then becoming aware of how silly they must sound, like two inexperienced high school girls babbling on to this independent college woman, she lowered the pitch of her voice and tried to sound calm. "So do you know where the guys are?"

"At the hospital."

Christy felt as if a huge fist had just reached into her chest and squeezed the air out of her lungs. She found just enough breath to ask, "Is it Todd? Is he okay?"

"It was Rick," the girl replied.

The fist released her lungs, and she let out a wobbly sigh.

"Rick?" Katie said, looking like the invisible fist had just grabbed her by the heart. "Is he okay? What happened?"

"I'm sure he'll be fine. He hurt his arm when the guys were in the pool this afternoon. They were doing handsprings off the diving board, and Rick had some kind of competition going. He twisted his arm the wrong way."

"Sounds like Rick," Christy said under her breath.

"We'd better go to the hospital," Katie said, urgently returning to her mission of retrieving the car keys. "Do you know how to get there?"

"I don't think it would help much for you to go. Todd and

Doug took him more than an hour ago. I imagine they'll be back before you could get to the hospital."

"Got it!" Katie said, popping the door open and reaching for the keys. "Are you sure we shouldn't go?"

"I guess you could, if you wanted. I think they'll be back any minute, though. Or you could stay here and help me with dinner. I told the guys I'd have a spaghetti feast for them when they came back."

Christy turned to Katie, who still looked worried, and said, "The way this afternoon has been, I don't think you and I should be driving around San Diego trying to find the hospital. It seems to me we should stay here and help . . . ," she paused, realizing she didn't know the girl's name.

"I'm Stephanie," the girl filled in the blank for her. "And you must be Christy. I've heard a lot about you."

Christy felt her cheeks warming. "And this is Katie," she said.

"Did you happen to hear anything about me, say, from Rick maybe?" Katie asked.

Stephanie smiled a delicate, mysterious smile. Her face reminded Christy of a soft, pink apple blossom.

"Rick has lots to say about a lot of things. Perhaps he has mentioned you."

Christy glanced at Katie, concerned about the way her friend might take such an answer. A bit of a relationship had sprouted between Rick and Katie at the Rose Parade on New Year's Day, but that was five months ago. Katie had tried to further the relationship since then, but nothing had brought Rick back into her life. This weekend was designed to be the test. Christy could tell it hurt Katie that Rick hadn't spoken of her the way Todd had talked about Christy. But then Christy and Todd had almost two years of relational history to draw from.

"I guess we'll stay then," Katie decided, locking the door again, this time with the keys in her hand.

"Bring up your suitcases," Stephanie said. "You're both staying with me tonight. I'm in number ten. Two doors down from the nut house."

"Thanks for letting us sleep at your place," Christy said. "Todd told me he would make arrangements with one of the girls in the complex. I'm just glad you're the first one we ran into!"

"It's pretty quiet around here," Stephanie explained as they headed for her place. "School was out more than a week ago, and almost everyone has gone home for the summer. I work at the same restaurant as the guys. The Blue Parachute. Did they tell you about it?"

Christy nodded. Katie looked a little left out.

Stephanie unlocked her apartment door. "We all agreed when we took the jobs to stay until June so the restaurant could switch over to its summer help. Here we are," she announced, opening the door and revealing a tidy, nicely decorated apartment.

"Welcome to my humble home. Please make yourselves comfortable. My roommate left yesterday, so the empty room is all yours."

Christy and Katie lugged their bags into the bedroom on the right. The only thing in the room was a standing lamp in the corner.

"Todd didn't tell me we were supposed to bring sleeping bags," Christy whispered.

"I'll ask Rick if I can borrow his," Katie said. "Maybe Stephanie has one too."

Soft, classical music floated into their room, and the girls followed its sound back to the living room where Stephanie had turned on the stereo.

"This is a really cute apartment," Christy said, surveying the blue and white striped futon couch, the hanging lamps covered with blue and peach flowered fabric, and the variety of intriguing pictures on the walls.

One of the larger pictures caught Christy's eye. A young woman was wearing a long, pink, lacy dress, with her hair puffed on top of her head like a cloud. From the surrounding garden scenery, it looked like summer, and the woman was seated on a bench, wishfully looking out to the ocean.

"I love this picture!" Christy said.

The scene stirred something inside her. It was the hint of another time and place. A time when women were praised for looking feminine and being dreamers. A place for tea parties and parasols and wearing long, white, lacy gloves for a stroll in the garden.

I think I was born a hundred years too late.

"Thanks," Stephanie called out from the kitchen, where she was unloading her groceries. "Would you two like something to drink? Have you ever had iced ginseng tea?"

The two girls made a face at each other and cautiously approached the kitchen.

"Whatever you have is fine," Christy said graciously.

"Do you happen to have any Coke? Pepsi?" Katie ventured.

"I don't," Stephanie said. "But I'm sure the guys do. I have a key to their place. Do you want to go over and get some?"

"Are you sure it's okay?" Katie asked.

"I'm sure they won't mind. They gave me the key because they kept locking themselves out. Sometimes those guys seem like Peter Pan and the Lost Boys, and they think I'm their Wendy."

Christy liked Stephanie. She seemed awfully sweet. There was an international flair about her, and she was intriguing.

"Come on," Katie said. "Let's go raid the guys' refrigerator. This ought to be fun."

Stephanie handed them the key. As Christy turned it in the guys' door, she looked over her shoulder to make sure they hadn't returned.

"Doesn't this feel sneaky to you?" she asked Katie.

"Yeah, it's fun! Let's freeze their underwear or something."

"Katie!"

"What? It was only a suggestion."

"Where do you come up with these things?" Christy asked as the door opened, and the two of them glanced around the room. "What a mess!" Christy said under her breath.

The two spies entered slowly and took in the full spectrum. To their right, in the kitchen area, were folding chairs at a card table with a box of sugary cereal in the middle. Surrounding the box were three bowls with puddles of pink, soured milk from the dissolved cereal. A half-full liter bottle of generic cola stood next to the cereal box.

"I feel like Goldilocks," Christy whispered.

"Me too," Katie said with a giggle. "Let's see where the three bears sleep."

"Katie!"

"I'm not going to steal their underwear, I promise. I was only kidding. Come on. I'm curious."

They stuck close together as they made their way through the living room, which hosted a long brown couch, an overstuffed plaid chair, a small TV balanced precariously on a cement block bookcase, and an old trunk covered with surfing magazines, which served as a coffee table in the center of the room.

"Very stylish," Katie quipped. "It's the ever popular 'early-slob' decor."

Christy noticed Todd's orange surfboard in the corner, serving as a coat rack at the moment.

"This must be Rick and Doug's room," Katie said, peeking around the half-opened door on the right.

Two unmade beds hugged the walls. The floor between the beds was covered with clothes, books, empty potato chips bags, and a neon yellow Frisbee. A bike was tucked behind the door, and a guitar was propped up in the corner with a Padres baseball cap balanced on top.

"How can you tell?" Christy asked.

"Easy. The guitar is Doug's, and the bike is Rick's."

"Todd plays the guitar too," Christy said.

"This doesn't look like Todd. Come on. Let's see what the room of a surf rat looks like."

Christy felt hesitant to follow Katie. Doug and Rick were two of the neatest dressers she knew. If they could live in such a messy room and appear so tidy in public, then what would "Mr. Casual's" room look like?

"Christy," Katie called from the bedroom on the right, "you have to see this!"

Christy looked into Todd's room but couldn't believe what she saw.

The room was immaculate.

"Do you really think this is Todd's room?" she whispered.

"What's that?" Katie asked, pointing to a peculiar box in the center of the room. Standing only a few inches up from the floor, the large, wooden-framed box was covered with a rippled sheet and had a neatly folded blanket at one end.

"It's too small to be a waterbed."

Katie poked it, and the substance under the sheet gave way. "It feels like . . ." She pulled back the corner of the sheet and announced, "It is; it's sand. I don't believe it!"

Christy joined in the examination and felt Todd's unique sand mattress.

Katie started to laugh. "Only Todd would sleep in a giant kitty litter box!"

"I'll bet it's really comfortable," Christy said, quickly coming to his defense. "After sleeping out on the Hawaiian beach while he was in the surfing competition, he's probably more comfortable in the sand than on a mattress."

Katie turned to Christy and smiled, her bright green eyes doing a merry dance. "Like I said, only Todd."

Christy noticed a grouping of pictures and posters on the wall behind the bed. In the center was a poster of a waterfall on Maui where Todd, Christy, her friend Paula, and her little brother David had spent a day last summer. The three other posters were surfing shots. A half-dozen photographs surrounded the posters, all stuck to the wall with thumb tacks.

"They're all of you," Katie said. "Look at that. All these pictures are of you."

Christy was amazed. Over the years she had sent Todd a picture here or there, but she never would have guessed he would save them or would create a place of honor for them.

"Isn't that your picture from the eighth grade?" Katie asked, pointing to a wallet-size picture at the top.

"Oh, no, look at that! It's from ninth grade. That is such a pathetic picture. I must have sent that to him right after we met. That's about the time he left Newport Beach and went to live with his mom in Florida."

Katie took a close look at the small photo and then looked at

Christy. "May I just say you've improved over the years?"

Christy laughed at the little-girl expression on her face in the picture. Her hair was long then, almost to her waist, and hung straight down in an uncomplimentary fashion.

"This one must be tenth grade," Katie said. "That's when I met you, when you moved to Escondido. Look how different you looked with short hair! It was too short then, if you ask me. I like the way you wear your hair now."

Christy had been growing her hair out ever since she had let her aunt talk her into whacking it all off the summer before her sophomore year. Now, at the end of her junior year, it was past her shoulders.

"I can't believe Todd has all these pictures. I don't even re-member sending some of them to him," Christy said. "I do re-member this one, though," she said, pointing to a snapshot of the two of them at the Hawaiian waterfall in the poster.

"Listen," Katie said. "Is that them coming?"

Christy heard the thump of heavy footsteps coming down the corridor outside the apartment. They both heard loud, male voices approaching.

"Do you think they'll go to Stephanie's first?" Christy asked.

"Why? They don't know we're here. It sounds like they're coming inside. Quick, hide!" Katie dove for Todd's closet. The minute she opened it, a mound of clothes and junk tumbled out, showering her with damp swimming trunks and a sprinkling of sand.

"Ewww!"

"Shhh," Christy said. "They're coming in!"

Katie quickly stuffed the clothes back into the closet and whispered, "What should we do?"

"Act natural!" Christy said, standing perfectly still in the middle of Todd's room, her hands behind her back and a nervous grin pasted on her face.

They could hear the front door of the apartment open. One of the guys said, "Hey, it was unlocked. Is somebody here?"

"What should we say?" Katie asked under her breath. She took her place by Christy's side, looking like her mirror image, with hands behind her back and a goofy grin frozen on her face.

Christy could tell by the pounding footsteps that the three bears were about to discover them. There was no way to look anything other than stupid.

"Katie, think of something, quick!"

CHAPTER TWO

Mr. Gizmo

As Christy and Katie heard the guys coming down the hallway toward Todd's bedroom, Katie, quick thinker that she was, shouted, "Surprise!"

Christy quickly joined in. "Surprise!"

She spotted Todd's screaming, silver-blue eyes opened wide in surprise. He started to laugh, and in two giant steps, he had his arms around Christy. She hugged him back, her ear pressed against his chest where his deep laugh rumbled. She wondered if he could feel her heart about to pound out of her chest.

"You sure surprised us!" Todd said, giving Katie a quick hug. He ran his fingers through his bleached blond hair.

Doug and Rick followed with hugs for both the girls. There were lots of explanations and laughter and lots of sympathy, especially on Katie's part, when they saw the bandage around Rick's sprained wrist.

"So Stephanie knows you're here?" Doug asked. He stood a little taller than Todd, but not as tall as Rick.

Seeing the three of them all lined up, Christy realized Rick was the most striking of the three. His dark, wavy hair, deep brown eyes, and athletic build had been the obsession of many girls at her high school last year, including her. No wonder Katie couldn't get Rick out of her mind. In any room, any situation, his looks commanded full attention.

If Christy hadn't dated Rick for a short time and experienced some of the not-so-pleasant sides of his personality, she too might have been staring at him now the way Katie was.

As far as Christy was concerned, she would choose Todd or Doug over Rick any day. Katie, she knew, would have to come to her own conclusion on that, just as Christy had.

"We were supposed to be raiding your refrigerator for soda," Katie explained, her blunt-cut copper hair swishing dramatically as she looked to Christy for support and then back at the guys. "Only we thought we would do a little room inspection first. We were pleased to find your 'kitty litter' box so nice and clean. Only one question, though. Where's the cat?"

Doug started to laugh at Katie, who was pointing to Todd's bed as though she were a game-show model showing off the show-case of prizes.

Doug had a clean-cut appearance, with his sandy blond hair that always looked as though he had just had it cut. He was good-looking in a boyish way and appeared younger than his twenty years. The most outgoing of the three guys, Doug was known for his hugs, which he gave out generously.

"Try it," Todd challenged Katie. "Lie on it and see how it feels."

Katie, ever the good sport, lay down on the sand bed as they all watched. She wiggled her back until she had formed the perfect support.

Folding her hands over her stomach, she said, "Okay, I'm convinced. This is the perfect bed. Did you invent this, Todd?"

"Not much to invent," he said. "A couple of boards, a couple of sand bags, and a blanket. I don't think the patent office would recognize it as a true invention."

"You didn't go in our room, did you?" Doug asked.

Katie and Christy exchanged glances.

Christy said, "We'll never tell!"

"I told you we should have picked up," Doug said to Rick out of the side of his mouth. "Todd had the right idea."

"What do you mean?" Rick said. "Todd just threw everything in his closet."

"We could have done that too," Doug said with a smile. "Might have impressed them."

"If I'm going to impress anyone," Rick said confidently, "it's going to be with my other attributes. Not with my housekeeping skills."

"Obviously," Katie said under her breath.

"I heard that," Rick said.

Christy watched carefully to see if anything might be starting up between the two of them.

"And which of your fine attributes are you going to start with?" Katie teased, getting up from the sand bed. "Perhaps your wonderfully coordinated skills on the diving board?"

"No," Rick countered quickly, "my skill at keeping girls off balance." As he said it, he gently pushed Katie with his good hand so that she toppled back into the sand pit.

Katie gave Rick a firm look of indignation, but Christy could tell Katie was feeling honored to have been the object of Rick's teasing.

"Todd," Katie asked from where her bottom was planted in the sand, "may I show your roommate a handful of your bed? In his face?"

"It's up to you," Todd said. "I'm going to see if Stephanie

needs any help with that spaghetti.''

"I'll join you," Christy said.

"I'm right behind you," Doug echoed. "What did you need from our fridge? Drinks and what else?"

Christy and Doug followed Todd to the kitchen, leaving Katie and Rick alone. She could hear Katie's muffled voice teasing Rick and then laughter. So far, so good.

Doug opened the old, gold-colored refrigerator and pulled out a couple liter bottles of soda. The rest of the refrigerator's contents looked as if they might fit nicely into the penicillin family of molds.

"Do you guys ever clean out this thing?" Christy ventured.

"Todd did once, didn't you, Todd? Couple of weeks ago, I think," Doug said. "We're all moving out next week. We'll dump everything then."

Todd was standing by the card table, shaking the box of cereal and looking inside. "Did you guys find the toy yet?"

"Don't think so," Doug said. "What is it this time?"

"Some kind of plastic gizmo that walks down windows," Todd said, his face brightening as he stuck his hand inside.

Christy could tell by the way his one dimple appeared on his right cheek that he had found the treasure and was pretty pleased with himself.

"Check it out," Todd said, tearing the clear wrapper from the gizmo with his teeth and tossing the critter against the window. "It's Mr. Gizmo!"

Sure enough, Mr. Gizmo walked. The first row of tiny suction cups on its feet stuck to the smooth window for a moment and then released as the next row hung tight. It gave the appearance of "walking" down the glass.

"Cool," Todd said, sticking the treasure in the pocket of his shorts. "You two ready to go?"

"We're ready," Rick answered, appearing in the living room with Katie in a headlock with his good arm. With his bandaged hand he pinched her cheek.

Christy would have been furious if Rick had ever treated her like that. Katie gave every indication she was in heaven. *Maybe they are good for each other.*

The group filed out the door, and Christy noticed a large mayonnaise jar half-filled with coins on a shelf. Doug had told her about that jar. The guys used it to collect money for a young boy they supported in Kenya. Christy had seen a letter that ten-year-old Joab had written to Doug and the guys. She also knew Doug carried a picture of Joab in his wallet and showed it around as if he were the proud big brother.

"Guess what, Doug?" Christy said as Todd locked the door and they followed Rick and his crutch, Katie, down the corridor. "I wrote to the organization that set you up as a sponsor for Joab. My family and I adopted a four-year-old girl from Brazil. Her name is Anna Maria. I never thanked you for giving me the information. So thanks."

"Awesome!" Doug said, slipping his arm around Christy and giving her a quick Doug-hug. "Isn't it amazing how little it takes to feed and clothe those kids?"

"Steph," Rick called out at the door of apartment number ten, "open up! It's the Rickster. I've come to collect your sympathy."

"Yeah, right," Stephanie said, opening the door and giving Rick a playfully disgusted look. "Like I'd ever give you anything, least of all sympathy."

Rick let go of Katie and stepped into the apartment, continuing his lively flirtation with Stephanie as if Katie didn't exist.

"Aren't you going to kiss it and make it better?" Rick asked, holding out his sore paw to her with a pout on his handsome face.

"When pigs fly!" Stephanie tossed back at him.

Rick then wrapped his good arm around Stephanie's shoulders and walked into the living room, still pleading for her sympathy.

Oh, no, look out, Katie! When you put your heart out there on the edge of the wall, it doesn't take much for it to do the ol' Humpty-Dumpty crash.

Katie seemed fine. She went in the kitchen and stirred the pot of spaghetti sauce as if she had been asked to do so. Christy had never admired her resiliency more than she did at that moment.

"We brought some sodas," Doug said, offering the two bottles for Stephanie to see before he placed them on the counter.

"Want me to finish making this garlic bread?" Todd asked, picking up a knife and slicing the loaf of French bread where Stephanie had left off.

"Sure," Stephanie said, turning her back to Rick and joining them in the kitchen. "Christy, could you help me get a salad going?"

Todd, Stephanie, Christy, and Katie all worked together in the narrow kitchen while Doug and Rick planted themselves on the sofa and turned on the TV.

"Their home away from home—in front of my TV," Stephanie said to Christy, motioning to Rick and Doug over her shoulder. "If you ever want to make sure you have lots of attention from guys in your apartment complex, all you have to do is be the only who subscribes to cable."

"I'll remember that," Katie said, helping Todd wrap the pungent garlic bread in foil. Katie waved her hand above the bread to clear the strong aroma and asked sarcastically, "Are you sure you used enough garlic, Todd?"

"It's good that way. You'll see. It's my secret recipe. Butter, mayonnaise, and lots of garlic."

"And only three thousand calories a slice," Stephanie said with a wink as she turned on the oven and handed Katie a cookie sheet for the bread. "It's good. Trust me. Todd's made it before. That's why the kitchen wallpaper is starting to peel."

Even though she knew Stephanie was kidding, Christy glanced at the wallpaper. There was nothing wrong with it. Every little peach heart stood in place.

Christy liked the way Stephanie used lots of hearts in decorating the kitchen. She especially liked the heart-shaped basket hanging on a nail above the sink. Peach ribbons were strung through the sides with a bunch of silk flowers attached at the bottom.

Christy liked colorful decor like that and thought how fun it would be to decorate her own apartment some day.

When they all sat down to eat a little while later, she decided one day she would have straight-back wooden chairs with padded cushions at her kitchen table, just like Stephanie's. And she would serve her guests on blue and white dishes, just like Stephanie.

Todd was right. The bread was delicious, as was the spaghetti and everything else. The conversation around the tightly packed table remained lively. Everything about this gathering made Christy feel grown-up and included in her circle of college friends. It felt completely different from being a sixteen-year-old living at home with her parents and eleven-year-old brother.

Oh, no, Christy suddenly remembered, *I promised I would call home as soon as we arrived!*

"May I use your phone?" she quietly asked Stephanie.

"Sure. There's one in my bedroom."

Christy slipped into Stephanie's room and closed the door. She felt awful for being so forgetful.

Mom answered, and Christy quickly explained about the guys not being there, the keys being locked in the car, meeting Stephanie, and Rick's sprained wrist. When she finished, there was an uncomfortable pause on the other end.

"Honest, Mom, that's what happened, and that's why I didn't think to call."

"Oh, I believe you," Christy's mother answered. "It's just that with all that has gone on during the last few hours, I'm not sure I'm ready for all the adventures you may face between now and when you come home tomorrow night."

"Mom," Christy said, trying her best to sound mature and responsible, "there's nothing to worry about. I'm really sorry I didn't call sooner. Everything is fine, and I'm sure the rest of our visit will be uneventful. I'll call you tomorrow before we leave to drive home. I really appreciate you and Dad letting me spend time with my friends like this."

"Well, have a good time and remember all the things we talked about."

"I will, Mom. Don't worry. I'll be fine."

Christy sat for a moment on the edge of Stephanie's bed after she hung up. She couldn't help feeling a little like a baby in this group where all of them were living on their own except Katie and her. Katie's parents not only let her go on this trip but they also gave her the car with a full tank of gas and told her to have fun. Katie didn't have to check in with them.

Christy felt fully aware of that ever-present, invisible rope that connected her to her parents. The older she became, the more rope they let out and the more they encouraged her to go exploring on independent experiences like this overnight trip to San Diego. Still, that invisible rope kept her anchored to them. In situations like this, when she had to check in, the rope seemed to pull awfully tight, right around her stomach.

Then she had a thought that was even more sobering. *Really soon I'm going to be eighteen. I'll be in college and living on my own like Stephanie. What will it feel like for that rope to be cut?*

Christy decided to be grateful for the linkage while she had it. She felt secure, knowing the invisible rope to her parents was intact and taut. It would be gone soon enough.

Katie doesn't seem to have any ropes attached to her, Christy thought. *That must feel scary. As if you didn't know for sure if someone is going to be there to pull you in if you go too far.*

Joining the others, Christy pitched in and helped to clear the table and dry the dishes. Doug washed and Todd put them away.

"Look how lovely my hands are after using this new dish soap!" Doug said in a high-pitched voice, holding up his bubble-covered hands.

"How's this for squeaky clean?" Doug rubbed his finger over the back of one of his plates, continuing to act out his commercial.

"Wait, I have an idea," Todd said, snatching the plate Christy was drying. He pulled Mr. Gizmo from his pocket and threw it on the back of the plate. Mr. Gizmo started to walk down the plate.

Doug whistled his applause. "Good show, good show! Now try it on the refrigerator."

Todd did, and it worked again.

More cheers and whistles came from Doug, and Christy joined him with eager applause.

"The oven door," Doug challenged.

Mr. Gizmo met the challenge.

"Now the true test—can he walk on the ceiling?"

Todd tossed Mr. Gizmo onto the ceiling.

Fwaaap! He stuck perfectly, but he didn't walk. He didn't move at all.

"Boo! Hiss!" Doug appraised the immobile Mr. Gizmo.

"What are you guys doing in there?" Stephanie called from the living room.

"It's the Mr. Gizmo Olympics," Doug said. "And our favorite contender just experienced a major setback."

"I'll get it down," Todd offered, pulling over one of Stephanie's chairs with the flowered cushions.

"Don't stand on that," Christy scolded. "It's too nice to stand on."

"What do you suggest," Doug asked, "waiting for gravity to keep its law?"

Christy had an idea. She twirled the dish towel in her hand and snapped it toward the ceiling, just missing Mr. Gizmo. But the towel gave off a loud, cracking sound.

"Good thinking," Doug said, snatching another towel from the handle of the refrigerator and snapping it in the air. "Take *that*, you Mr. Gizmo, you!"

"You missed," Todd told him, reaching for a towel and giving it a try.

Before Christy knew what was happening, she was stuck in the middle of a towel-snapping war between Doug and Todd.

"Whoa! Wait a minute! How did I get between you guys?" she cried out, trying to break loose from the circle. It was no use. They had her surrounded.

Christy began to snap them back, but they were faster and more experienced at this. On impulse, she scooped both her hands into the bountiful soap bubbles in the sink. With a mound of the white fluff, she glanced at Doug and then at Todd.

"Okay, who's going to get it first?"

Before she could decide which one to "suds," Doug slid his hand under hers and pushed the whole mound into her face. Some of it went up her nose.

Christy let out a squeal and wiped the suds from her eyes in time to see Doug and Todd giving each other a snap of their towels over her head. Just as their towels came down, so did Mr. Gizmo—right on the top of Christy's head.

They all started laughing and Todd grabbed the toy out of her hair.

Just then someone knocked on the door. As Christy blew bubbles out of her nose, seven college students entered the apartment and greeted everyone. Christy reached for the towel in Doug's hand and finished mopping up, feeling embarrassed.

"You okay?" Doug asked, pulling her over to the corner of the kitchen.

"I think so," Christy said, looking up at him. "Did I get it all?"

"Here," Doug said, taking the towel and gently wiping under the corner of her right eye. He then smoothed down the top of her hair where Mr. Gizmo had landed.

"Good as new," he announced. Taking her by the hand, he said, "Don't be shy. Come meet the rest of the God-Lovers."

Christy smiled and greeted the three girls and four guys who had just arrived. She tried to think of a way to remember all their names.

There was another knock on the door, and two more girls entered. One of them was really outgoing as well as gorgeous. She went right to Rick and asked about his bandaged wrist. She soon made up for the lack of sympathy Rick had received from the rest of them.

Everyone found a seat on the floor or by pulling over one of the kitchen chairs. No one said it was time to start. They all sort of fell into place as if this was a familiar habit for all of them. Christy noticed that Todd had disappeared, and she wasn't sure where to sit. Katie was right next to Rick on the couch with the blond on his other side and her friend next to her. Doug seemed to be in charge. Stephanie was on the floor talking with one of the guys.

Christy slipped into an open spot by the wall near the front. A lifetime of familiar "left-out" feelings joined her in the corner and kept her company. As long as she was wrapped up in those feelings, she couldn't make the effort to start chatting with anyone. She was the visitor. They should greet her. No one did.

Todd came back in with his guitar and Doug's. The two of them sat on chairs in front of the TV and took a few minutes to tune their instruments.

Three more girls showed up, and one of them wedged in next to Christy.

"Hi, I'm Beth," she said.

"I'm Christy."

"Nice to meet you. Are you visiting?"

"Yes," was all Christy could explain before Doug spoke up.

"I'm glad you guys are all here tonight," he said. "As you know, most of the God-Lovers have taken off for the summer. This is our last time together until next fall. I thought it would be good if we spent some time thanking God for the awesome stuff He's done in our lives this past year."

Todd started to play his guitar, and Doug joined him in strumming Rich Mullins' song, "Our God Is an Awesome God." Somehow Christy knew that would be Doug's favorite song since "awesome" was his favorite word.

She knew the song and sang along with the others, feeling a little amazed that so many college students were sitting there, openly singing their hearts out to God. One guy toward the front had his eyes closed and both arms slightly lifted up in a gesture of praise to God.

Christy couldn't explain it, but somehow after that first song and then listening to Todd open in prayer, she felt all her defenses dissolve. The people in this room were Christians. All of them seemed to be there to worship God. These college students were some of her brothers and sisters in Christ. Even if she never saw them again, she would spend eternity with them in heaven. She felt included in God's family.

Doug started to strum the next song, which Christy didn't know. Instead of feeling left out, she quietly closed her eyes and bowed her head to listen while everyone else sang.

> *Eyes have not seen. Ears have not heard.*
> *Neither has it entered into the heart of man*
> *The things God has planned*
> *For those who love Him.*

For two hours they sang and prayed and talked about what was going on in their lives. Then Doug read some Bible verses and talked about waiting on God and trusting Him for the future. Everyone seemed to get into what he had to say, especially since most of them were taking off in different directions the next week. Not many of them knew what the future held.

After Todd closed in prayer, everyone started to visit with each other. Christy, feeling warmed by the sweet spirit of the group, walked around and met everyone she hadn't been introduced to before. She had never been this outgoing, and to her surprise, it wasn't that hard.

"Do you want to come out to coffee with us?" Beth asked. "A bunch of us are going. Your friend Katie said she would come, and I'm sure Stephanie is coming."

All Christy's warm feelings disappeared. One of her agreements with her parents for this trip was that she wouldn't go out after dark. It seemed like such a silly rule now. If her parents had been there, they would have seen how responsible all these people were.

Still, if she went without asking, she would be breaking her agreement. Maybe she could call and explain the situation, and they would understand and give her permission to go.

Christy glanced at the clock on the kitchen wall: 9:45. She knew her parents were probably in bed. Her dad worked at a dairy and had to be up early every morning. He usually went to bed before she did. It would *not* be good to call and wake him to ask a favor like this. Still, if she didn't ask . . .

"Come on, Christy. We're going to The Blue Parachute," Katie said enthusiastically. "Grab your purse and let's go."

Todd was talking to some people in the kitchen. It would help if she knew whether or not he was going.

"Ready?" Doug asked, coming alongside her. "We're all going. You want to ride with Todd or me?"

"I . . . I'm not sure," Christy said. She hated having to make decisions like this. Especially when she knew that either way she would come up the loser. Which was the worst to lose? Her friends' approval or her parents' trust?

CHAPTER THREE

Elephants, Monkeys, and Snakes

"Okay, I'll go," Christy said, regretting her impulsive words the minute she said them.

My parents will never know. I won't tell them. We're only going to a restaurant. What could happen? They would understand if they met these guys.

"I have room," Todd called out to Doug and Christy, "if you both want to ride with me. Stephanie is going with me."

Christy numbly followed the rest of the group down to the parking lot and watched Katie laugh and joke with Rick on their way to his classic red Mustang. She was one of three girls riding with Rick.

Todd opened the side door of his old Volkswagen bus called "Gus." Glancing at Christy, he asked, "Are you okay?"

"Sure," she answered quickly, certain her guilt showed all over her face. She never had been good at sneaking around. She was especially bad at lying.

Doug moved in for a closer look into Christy's eyes. "No, you're not," he said. "Something's wrong. What is it, Christy?"

"It's just that I had an agreement with my parents that I wouldn't go out after dark once Katie and I got here. I know if they were here, it would be different. They would let me go."

"But they're not here," Todd said, sliding shut the van's door.

"We'll stay too," Doug said.

"I have stuff to make banana splits," Stephanie said. "Not enough for the whole group, but it should be enough for the four of us."

"You guys don't have to stay," Christy said. "I'll stay, and you guys go."

"Why would we?" Todd asked.

"Don't worry about it, Christy," Stephanie said. "These guys don't care where they go as long as food is involved. It'll give us a chance to talk, and that will be nice."

Todd flagged down Rick, who was about to peel out of the parking lot. He jogged over to Rick's window and, bending down, explained the situation to Rick. Christy could feel Rick's gaze as he looked past Todd at her.

She was sure he was remembering all the rules her parents had laid down for her when they were dating.

That's right, everyone gawk at me, she thought. *Here I am: Christy Miller, the biggest baby in the world!*

Katie's lighthearted laughter rippled into the air. Todd patted the side of the car three times, the way a cowboy pats his horse's side. With a squeal of tires, Rick peeled out, hurrying to catch up with the other cars that had already left.

As the four of them headed back for Stephanie's apartment, Christy felt an overwhelming urge to keep apologizing. "I'm really sorry, you guys. Thanks for doing this for me."

Doug slipped his arm around Christy and said, "What kind of God-Lovers would we be if we didn't support you when you have an opportunity to honor your parents?"

"I still feel bad for holding you guys back. Really, if you want to go, that's fine. I could stay here by myself."

"Christy," Todd said, "shake it off." He shook both his hands in front of her for emphasis. "You're the only one making a big deal of this."

She might have felt reprimanded or embarrassed by such a comment from someone else. Not from Todd. She could take it from him, and when she did, something inside her calmed down.

Stephanie welcomed them all back into her kitchen, where they set to work creating masterpiece banana splits, topped off with a whipped-cream fight.

Stephanie started to talk about how she was going back to San Francisco next week to spend the summer working at her father's computer store.

"Her parents came over from China," Doug explained to Christy. "It's an awesome story. Her dad was handed a Chinese Bible by some guy who smuggled it into the country. It was the first time he had ever heard of the Bible. He read it and gave his heart to the Lord and then found some other Christians who were meeting in an underground church. That's where he met Stephanie's mom."

Stephanie jumped in. "Actually, they had met at the university, but neither of them knew the other was a believer."

"That's amazing," Christy said, licking the chocolate sauce off the back of her spoon. "How did they end up in San Francisco?"

Stephanie launched into the story of all the hardships her parents endured in trying to get out of China. "They were extra motivated when my mom was pregnant with me. They had to leave before the pregnancy became obvious."

Todd leaned over and explained to Christy, "Mandatory abortion. It's China's way of population control. They already had one kid, and that's the allotment per family."

Christy's eyes grew wide. "You mean you would have been aborted if your parents had stayed there?"

Stephanie nodded.

Christy had heard vague stories before of how hard life was in other countries, but she had never met anyone who had "escaped" and come to America.

"So obviously your parents made it out of the country," Christy said.

"I was born four months after they arrived at my uncle's in San Francisco, so all I know are the dramatic stories. The hard part now is that here we are in a country where we're free to worship God, and one of my younger brothers wants nothing to do with Christianity. I think that's been harder on my parents than anything else they've been through."

Christy thought about Stephanie's words later that night as she lay on the floor in her sleeping bag. Katie and the others hadn't returned yet, and Christy couldn't sleep. She felt as if she had grown up more that night than she had during her entire junior year of high school. The conversation with Stephanie had sobered her and caused her to realize how easy it was for her to be a Christian. She had never been challenged to do anything dangerous because of her faith.

Another part of the grown-up feeling came from being on her own, around college students. It made her feel independent, even though she hadn't been free to go out with everyone. Still, she was away from home, making new friends, and making good decisions. This was one night when growing up seemed like an honorable, wonderful experience.

Just then the front door to Stephanie's apartment opened. Through the half-open bedroom door, Christy could see Katie's silhouette standing there, whispering to Rick.

As Christy watched, Rick braced his good arm against the door frame and bent his head to be eye-level with Katie. Christy knew the move well. He had assumed the same stance with her more than once, right before he had kissed her. His hovering position had the effect of making the girl feel sheltered and yet vulnerable at the same time. She wasn't sure she could watch what would happen next.

But she did.

Rick kissed Katie. Instead of just receiving it, Katie looped her arms around Rick's neck and kissed him back. He pulled away slightly, and Katie removed her arms. Christy could hear muffled whispers, and then she saw Rick back up and wave good-bye.

"See you in the morning," Katie said softly.

She closed the door, and Christy could hear her humming.

Oh, Katie, I don't want Rick to break your heart!

Christy pretended to be asleep when Katie stepped into the room. She was sure it was well after midnight, and this would not be the time to have a heart-to-heart talk with her best friend.

I'll wait to see how things go between them tomorrow at the zoo. I haven't said one discouraging word to her about him yet. But if he treats her badly tomorrow, that's it. I'll do everything I can to break them up!

The next day, it took Christy more than an hour of walking around the zoo before she began to relax and quit working so hard at being super-sleuth.

Relaxing was difficult for several reasons. Rick appeared to be ignoring Katie, or at best, treating her as though she were an annoying little kid. Katie didn't seem to notice. She came on exceptionally loud and flirty. Twice Christy noticed Katie linking her arm with Rick's, but he didn't allow the connection to remain for long.

Plus Christy felt strained because there were five of them. Stephanie had to work, so Christy, Katie, Rick, Doug, and Todd went on the zoo adventure. A group of five was a lot harder to maneuver than four or even six.

By the flamingo lagoon at the main entrance, the group decided to ride the tram. Katie slid in next to Rick, Christy sat across from them, and Doug scooted in next to her. With no room for Todd, he had to sit on another seat next to some tourists who spoke only Japanese.

They disembarked and headed for the giraffe exhibit, the five of them mixed in with all the other tourists. It didn't feel as though they were their own group at all.

Katie reached the exhibit first and said, "Look at the baby giraffe! Isn't he cute?"

Doug stepped next to Christy, slipped his arm around her, and pointed to the grove of tall eucalyptus trees. "Look at that one giraffe twisting his neck around the tree. Doesn't he look like he's trying to play hide-and-seek, but the tree isn't quite thick enough?"

Christy laughed with Doug, but at the same time she was aware that Todd was walking off to the side by himself. Katie had again grasped Rick's arm and was stretching her neck, trying to entertain Rick with her giraffe impression.

Rick didn't look impressed.

Christy felt uneasy, as though it were up to her to make sure everyone was getting along and having a good time.

Stop it, she finally scolded herself in front of the koala exhibit as she watched a baby koala clinging to its mother. *You're not everyone's mother here, Christy. Relax and enjoy the day.*

"I want to see the elephants," Todd said. "Anybody have an idea which way we go?"

Doug pulled a folded zoo map from his back pocket and began to give directions. Rick pulled away from Katie and joined Doug, bending over the map.

"Do they still have the sea lion show?" Rick asked. "That was my favorite when I was a kid."

The three guys huddled around the map, and Christy cautiously sided up next to Katie. "I didn't get to ask you how everything went last night," she said in her best lighthearted voice. "Did you and Rick have a good time?"

Katie looked cross, but she answered calmly, "Yeah, it was great. We all had a good time."

Christy decided to venture a more direct statement. "You and Rick seem to be getting along okay."

Katie grabbed Christy by the arm and jerked her several yards away from the guys. She had tears in her eyes. "He doesn't like me, does he? Last night I thought something might be starting up between us, but all morning he's been pulling away from me and looking at me like I'm an idiot."

"You're not an idiot, Katie," Christy said.

"I feel like one. Why did I ever want to start up a relationship with him? Why is it so important for me to get him to like me?" Now she was crying.

Christy stood close to Katie so the guys couldn't see her crying. "It's okay, Katie. Really. You don't have to get Rick's approval. You don't have to try to make him like you. Just be yourself. You're wonderful just the way you are. If Rick recognizes that, great. If not, it's his loss."

Katie sniffed and wiped her damp cheeks with the back of her hand. Her bright green eyes looked like two emeralds at the bottom of a deep pool.

"Will you make me a promise?" Christy asked.

Katie nodded.

"Promise me you won't let Rick use you. He does that to girls, and you know it. I don't think he does it on purpose. He can't pass up a challenge, and sometimes I think once the challenge is gone, so is his attention. Do you know what I mean?"

"I know, I know. And you have every right to tell me these things, Christy. These are the same things I told you when you were dating him last year."

"Yes, I know," Christy said. "I didn't listen to you very well then, and I wouldn't blame you if you didn't listen to me now. But I still want you to promise me that you won't let Rick use you. You don't deserve to be treated badly by any guy."

Katie wiped away the last tear and peeked over Christy's shoulder at the guys. A smile returned to her face. "Look at those three," she said. "You'd think we were one of the zoo's attractions the way they're standing there cautiously observing us. If we stay here long enough they might throw peanuts!"

Christy looked at them and laughed with Katie. "Come on," she said. "Let's both try starting this adventure all over, okay?"

"Did you ever notice," Katie said, still eyeing the guys, who looked as though they didn't know how to approach this rare, female species, "how many things come in three's?"

"Like the three bears?" Christy asked.

"And three musketeers and three blind mice and," Katie added with a burst of laughter, "the three stooges!"

Christy motioned with a nod of her head as they started to walk back to the guys. "Which one do you want? Larry, Moe, or Curly?"

"You girls all right?" Doug asked, leaving the pack and approaching them.

"Sure," Katie said. "We were just discussing movie stars."

Christy tried to suppress her giggles and smiled at Todd, who shot back one of his warm, understanding smiles.

"How about visiting a famous star?" Doug asked. "It says a dancing elephant is here. Want to go visit him?"

"Sounds good," Katie said, ignoring Rick and smiling brightly at Doug. "Lead on into the jungle, O great trail master."

Doug and Katie led the way, and Christy followed, sandwiched in between Rick and Todd. The awkward fivesome dynamics returned.

"Why does he do that?" Katie asked a few minutes later when they stood watching the dancing elephant sway back and forth with his ankle chained to the ground. "Does that thing hurt him?"

"It doesn't seem to," Todd said. "I think he hears his own music and goes with it. Pretty cool, huh?"

Christy knew that when it came to someone hearing his own music and "going with it," Todd was king. He and the dancing elephant seemed to have a lot in common.

"How about some real animals," Rick said. "Where are all the lions and tigers? Don't they have any snakes here?"

"We already passed the lion, remember? He was snoozing. The monkeys are over this way," Doug said. "Let's check them out first."

Katie whispered to Christy, "Notice how each guy wants to see the animal he's most similar to?"

Christy nodded and smiled back.

"And did you notice how Rick wants to see some snakes?"

"I know! Remember how Jon, my boss at the pet store, used to compare Rick to a snake?"

"Well, I'm glad I came to my senses before he wrapped his coils around me!" Katie said a little louder.

Christy put her finger up to her lips and whispered, "Shhhhh!"

" 'Sssss' is more like it," Katie whispered back.

"What's with all the secrets, you two?" Doug asked.

Todd answered before Christy or Katie had a chance. "It's a girl thing. Makes them feel in control when they have secrets. You know they're whispering about us."

"You don't know that," Katie said, challenging Todd's philosophy. "We could be talking about something else."

"Like what?" Todd asked.

"Like, well . . . like anything," Katie answered with her hand on her hip. "Besides, you wouldn't know because, like you said, it's a girl thing."

Christy was glad they had stepped in front of the gorilla exhibit so the subject could change. A great, gray-black lowland gorilla sat on his haunches on a rock before them. His hands were folded under his chin, and he appeared to stare at all the zoo visitors.

"Look at that guy," Doug said. "You'd think he got up today just so he could sit there and watch the tourists walk by."

"He's not moving an inch," Todd said.

"I'll make him move," Rick said, picking up a peanut off the ground and tossing it at him.

"Don't throw things," Christy said. "Can't you read all the signs around here?"

"Look," Doug said, "he didn't flinch. The guy is a rock."

"The guy is smelly," Katie said, plugging her nose. "Can't you smell him?"

"I thought it was Doug," Rick teased.

"Ho, ho, very funny, Mr. Stuff-All-Your-Gym-Socks-Under-My-Bed."

Rick laughed. "I wondered what happened to all my socks."

"You guys," Todd said, reading the information sign in front of the gorilla, "it says here they have a 'distinct body odor that is unmistakable and quite offensive to humans.' "

"And then it has Doug's name at the bottom, right?" Rick said.

Doug slugged Rick on his unbandaged arm.

"Actually, it says, 'The odor does not stem from lack of cleanliness. In the wilds, the odor helps gorillas locate each other.' "

The guys all started to laugh as if it were the funniest thing they had ever heard.

"Must be a guy thing," Katie whispered to Christy.

"They are so weird! They'll laugh at anything," Christy whispered back.

"Come on," Rick said. "I want to see the snakes."

Christy and Katie broke into their own bout of laughter.

"Don't even try to understand them," Todd said, leading them on to the next exhibit. "It's a girl thing."

CHAPTER FOUR

Katie's Idea of a Good Time

Two weeks later, as Christy and Katie were driving home after their school yearbook-signing party, Katie asked, "What was with Fred? He made such a big deal about signing your yearbook. What did he write?"

"I don't know," Christy said, shaking her head and then motioning to her book in the back seat, "something like 'keep smiling and see you next year on the yearbook staff.' "

"Are you going to join the staff next year for sure?" Katie reached for the yearbook.

"I signed up, but I still don't know if I want to. I could, because I have that really good camera my uncle bought me for Christmas."

"I'm sure you could take better pictures than the ones Fred took this year," Katie said.

"Do you really think so?"

"Oh, I don't know," Katie said, opening her yearbook to the winter-break section and holding it up so Christy could see the center photo. "Let's see. There might be a little more stiff competition here than I realized. Fred did have a real talent for getting those candid shots."

"Get that picture out of my face," Christy said, refusing to look. Fred had taken a photo at a pizza place over Christmas break. It was enlarged as the center of the photo collage. The picture was of Christy sitting on the end of a booth, and Rick sitting halfway on her lap with his arm wrapped around her. Rick looked like a model, of course. Christy looked like someone who just had ice cubes slipped down her back.

Next to that picture was a small one of Katie goofing off that same night in the pizza place. She had Styrofoam cups on her ears and was pretending to be an elf. It was a much funnier photo than the one of Rick and Christy, and Christy wished the yearbook staff had used that one instead of hers to highlight the junior class collage.

"I guess if I join the yearbook staff I can at least have something to say about the pictures they use," Christy said.

"Might not be a bad idea after this picture." Katie flipped to the ski club page and pointed to the photo of Christy ramming into the ski instructor. Her skis had veered between his legs, and her face was buried in his chest.

"Why did they put my name under the picture?" Christy said with a moan. "No one would have known it was me if they hadn't done that."

"Don't complain. You have more pictures in here than I do."

"And that's a good thing?"

"Sure it is," Katie said. "You're becoming popular. I think it started when you turned down the cheerleader position last year and the whole school knew you did it just so Teri Moreno could take your place. Did you even want to try out again this year?"

"Not at all," Christy said. "Isn't that strange? Last year all I could think about was cheerleading, and now it's the last thing I'd want to do."

Christy pulled into the driveway of her house. "You want to come in for a while?"

"Sure. So what do you want to do?"

"What?" Christy asked as they walked up the steps to her front porch. The jasmine on the trellis was in bloom, and its sweet fragrance filled the air with memories.

"What do you want to do?" Katie repeated. "You don't want to go out for cheerleading, you might go on yearbook staff in the fall, but what do you want to do this summer?"

"Work, I guess. And go to the beach and spend time with you and Todd and everyone."

Christy opened the front door and greeted her mom, who was sitting on the couch watching TV and mending clothes.

"Hi, Christy. Hi, Katie." Mom spoke in a soft whisper.

The light from the floor lamp hit her dark, curly hair in such a way it made the gray strands shine like silver threads woven into a black woolen cap. "Dad's already asleep, and David should be."

"We'll be quiet," Christy promised.

It was difficult since their house was so small, and the three bedrooms all connected to the same hallway.

Once inside Christy's room with the door closed, Katie asked again what Christy planned to do during the summer. Christy scrutinized her friend's face before answering.

"Would I be correct in guessing you already have an idea of what we should do this summer?"

"How did you guess?"

"I can read you like a book, Katie Weldon. If I'm correct, right now you're thinking of something courageous, adventurous, daring, and slightly wacky."

"Who, me?"

Christy positioned her pillow against her headboard and

leaned back. "The last time you had that look on your face, you talked me into joining the ski club and going to Lake Tahoe."

"I'm not talking about skiing this time. I'm talking about summer camp."

Christy hadn't been to summer camp since she was in junior high. She liked the idea the minute Katie said it. "Where? When? With the youth group at church?"

"Yep. I signed us up last Sunday after you left. I wasn't sure you would like the idea, because I thought you might be planning on spending as much time with Todd as you could."

Christy let out a sigh. "You know, Katie, things never change with him. I feel like our relationship has hardly moved forward an inch since he came back from Hawaii. That was more than five months ago. Things seem the same as they were last year."

"At least he's consistent."

"Consistent? Boring is more like it."

"I wouldn't complain if I were you," Katie said. "Todd is there for you. He's always there for you. Shall we compare my last year of relationships?"

Katie lay on her back on the floor, counting on her fingers. "Let's see. There was Glen, the missionary kid from Ecuador who liked to talk on the phone, hugged me twice, and promised to write when he left for Quito two months ago. Of course, I haven't received a single word from him, and he must think I have no social life since I've written him four times."

"That's okay," Christy said. "I'm sure he'll write. Mail from South America probably takes a long time."

"Then there's the Rick experience. Kick me in the head if I ever start to like him again! Aside from one New Year's Eve kiss and one and a half kisses at Stephanie's apartment in San Diego, all I ever got from Rick was a severe blow to my self-esteem. I'm sure he thought it was better mine than his.

"There you have it," Katie concluded. "My sizzling love life! At least you have Todd. Nice, consistent, friend forever, won't mess with your mind, guards your heart, Todd."

"I guess," Christy reluctantly agreed.

Katie sat up and gave a tug on Christy's bedspread. "Stop your whining, girl! Can we have a reality check here? You have it great and don't know it."

Christy didn't try to explain her feelings to Katie. They were hers alone. Feelings of wanting to be romanced. When she had dated Rick, he had brought roses and said incredibly tender things. Todd never said mushy stuff or touched her hair and gazed in her eyes the way Rick had. But with Rick, it felt like a game, and she was the prize.

If Todd would only throw a little tender romance into their close, honest, consistent relationship, it would be perfect. He seemed to be holding back, and so of course, she held back too.

"Hello?" Katie said, waving her hand in the air to get Christy's attention. "Anybody home?"

"I'm sorry. What were you saying?"

"Summer camp. I think we should go to summer camp."

A warm sensation washed over Christy. A feeling of sitting around a campfire at night, of picking wildflowers, and of splashing into a sun-toasted lake. A feeling of mysteriously meeting someone in the woods. Someone new. Someone handsome and tender who would write her long, romantic letters and hold her hand in the moonlight.

"Excuse me," Katie said. "Am I, like, having a one-sided conversation here?"

"No, I'm listening. Summer camp. We're going to summer

camp. We're going to have a fantastic time at summer camp. I'm ready. Let's go!"

Katie's mouth turned up into a smile. "I don't know about you, Christy. I think you're asleep with your eyes open. Perhaps I'd better leave you alone to finish your dream without interruption."

Katie rose to her feet and said, "July fifth to the eleventh. Call Luke this week at church and tell him you agreed to go. He'll be glad. I'll see you later. Sweet dreams!"

Letting herself out, Katie left Christy with a swirl of exciting summer camp thoughts. She would have to ask her parents, request time off from work, and make sure she had enough clothes for the entire week. Maybe this summer would hold some adventure after all.

The next Sunday, Christy talked to Luke, their youth pastor, and asked some questions about the camp.

"It's called Camp Wildwood, and it's about two hours from here," the big, bearded, lovable youth pastor answered. "You'll have eleven girls in your cabin. Your tuition is paid, but I'm afraid I'll have to ask you to come up with twenty dollars for the transportation."

"That's no problem. And I already have the week off from work, so I'm all set."

Luke gave her an appreciative smile and said, "You know, Christy, I really am glad you're willing to do this."

"Willing? Are you kidding? I can't wait! I love going to camp."

"I'm glad. I think it'll be a good week. I want you to know how much I appreciate you and Katie for signing up. Not many of the other students are willing to give up a week of their summer."

"Well, they don't know what they're missing," Christy said. She thought it was great that the church was sponsoring the teens who wanted to go by paying for their tuition.

That afternoon, Todd came over, and they went to the beach. Even though summer was supposed to have arrived, it was chilly, and a thin mist of ocean fog hovered above the sand.

"Carlsbad is such a different beach from Newport," Todd commented as they sat together on a blanket and looked out at the waves. "It's hard to believe it's only sixty miles down the same Pacific coast from Newport. It feels as though I'm on the Atlantic."

"Why?" Christy asked, slipping on her sweatshirt and wrapping the end of the blanket around her bare feet. "Because it's so cold today?"

"No, it's the way the waves break. They seem to come in at a different angle here. I don't know. Could be the weather too. Although it's not unusual for it to be like this in June."

At Christy's home in Escondido, about a half-hour drive from Carlsbad, it had been warm and sunny when they had left. She had put on shorts and a T-shirt over her bathing suit. Her wise mother had tossed her a sweatshirt on her way out the door.

The wind whipped the sleeves of Todd's T-shirt. He seemed comfortable enough. Christy had never really noticed before, but the hair on Todd's legs looked white-blond and was super curly. He didn't even have goose bumps.

"I'm cold," Christy said.

Todd took his gaze off the ocean and looked at her in surprise. "You are?"

Christy smiled at his amazed expression and rubbed the goose bumps on her bare legs. "Yes, I am. I don't come with a built-in fur coat like you do to keep me warm." She playfully reached over and pulled one of the hairs on his leg.

"Ouch!" he said. Then noticing her smooth legs, he asked, "Why do girls do that, anyway? Shave their legs, I mean."

"So they'll look nice. You know, smooth and feminine."

"But then you get cold."

"Never mind," Christy said. Then she added, "Actually, we do it so that guys will feel sorry for us when we say we're cold, and they'll put their arms around us and warm us up."

"I have a better idea," Todd said, standing up and offering Christy his hand. "Let's walk."

Todd's hand felt strong and secure as they strolled down the beach together. Her legs were still cold, but inside she felt warm and content. That's how things had been between her and Todd for the last few months. More than brother and sister, not quite boyfriend and girlfriend.

She felt Todd's thumb rubbing the chain on the gold ID bracelet she wore on her right wrist. He had given it to her a year and a half ago with the word "Forever" engraved on it. It was Todd's promise that they would be friends forever. As it was, their relationship had gone through many ups and downs since they first met two summers ago. But Todd's promise had remained. He always treated her like a close friend. It was just that sometimes, like now, Christy wanted more.

"What are you thinking about?" she asked him.

"About Papua New Guinea," Todd answered. "I was wondering what angle the waves come in there."

What did I expect? Ever since I first met Todd, he's been dreaming of being a missionary to an island full of unreached natives. He's such a surfer boy, I bet if I cut him, he would bleed saltwater. Why did I think he would be thinking of me?

"What were you thinking?" he asked.

The question surprised her. Although she asked him for his thoughts often, he rarely asked her. Maybe Todd was becoming a little more like Christy as they spent more time together. She knew she was becoming a little more like him.

"I was thinking about us and wondering what the future held." One thing Christy had learned was to be honest with Todd.

There was a pause. Then Todd squeezed her hand and said, "Me too."

Christy felt her heart beat a little faster.

Todd stopped walking and turned to face her. The filtered sunlight shone on his face, illuminating his clear silver-blue eyes and highlighting his square jaw. His expression remained sober, and no dimple appeared on his right cheek.

"But you know what, Kilikina?"

Christy always melted when he called her by her Hawaiian name.

"If we spend all of today thinking about tomorrow, today will be gone, and we will have missed it."

Christy knew he was right. As much as she wished he would wrap his arms around her, hold her tight, kiss her hair, and tell her that all his future plans included her, she knew he wouldn't. Todd was reserved when it came to physical expression. It was part of his honesty. He once told her he would never purposefully "defraud" her.

When she asked what he meant, Todd said, "I won't deliberately arouse a desire in you that I can't follow through on honestly, before God."

She knew that if their relationship had been full of hugs and kisses and whispered secrets about their future, her desires for him would have been aroused past the point of no return.

As it was now, they could walk away from their relationship

today and, besides missing each other's close friendship, they would have no regrets about making promises they weren't able to keep or painful memories from having become too intimate.

"Then let's enjoy today," Christy said, her eyes smiling at Todd. "I'm glad we can be together. We'd better keep walking, though. I'm starting to get cold again."

Todd squeezed her hand and started down the beach. They spent the next two hours collecting shells, digging for sand crabs, and playing foot tag with the waves. It really was a wonderful afternoon.

When they arrived at home, Mom had tacos waiting for them and a message that Katie had called.

Christy didn't call Katie back until the next morning. The conversation was short, and Katie's news sent Christy back to bed on her first Monday of summer vacation.

"Christy," Mom called, tapping on her bedroom door, "are you okay?"

"Come on in, Mom. I'm bummed. Katie can't go to camp. Her parents won't let her because it's a church activity. Isn't that crazy? They let her take off and do all kinds of stuff you guys would never let me do, but they won't let her become too involved in church. It has to be hard for her, being the only Christian in her family."

"Do you still want to go?" Mom asked.

"Sort of. Not as much as before."

"Maybe we can call Luke and see if some other girls that you know are going," Mom suggested.

"Okay," Christy sighed. "But it won't be as much fun without Katie."

Christy didn't get around to calling Luke. When she saw him Sunday at church, she asked him who else was going to camp.

"You and Katie were the only two girls from the youth group."

Christy couldn't believe it. Their high school group had 250 people in it.

"I'm sorry Katie isn't going. We really need counselors. That's why I appreciated you both signing up."

"Counselors?" Christy squeaked. "Katie signed us up to be counselors?"

"For junior camp," Luke explained. "We need counselors for the fifth-grade girls. You thought Katie signed you up for high school camp? That isn't until the last week of August. Does this mean you want to drop out too?"

Something about the way Luke worded it made Christy feel as though she would be the flake of the year if she withdrew only a week before camp. Especially since Katie had backed out.

"No, I'll go," Christy said, trying to sound as though it didn't make much difference to her. "I have the time off from work, you need counselors. I'll go."

A huge grin spread over Luke's face. "Thanks, Christy. I knew I could count on you! It'll be a real stretching experience, you'll see."

"That's what I'm afraid of," Christy muttered.

The next Sunday, when she arrived in the church parking lot with her luggage and sleeping bag, she knew she wasn't up for this stretching experience. A sea of fourth- and fifth-grade kids ran through the mounds of luggage, yelling, hitting, tattling, and clearly presenting Christy with a glimpse into her next week.

It took more than an hour to organize the troops, load their luggage, and get everyone on the bus at one time. Christy sat in the seat right behind the driver, hoping to ignore most of the spit wads, smacking gum, and rude little boys. She realized her main goal this week would be to avoid getting gum in her hair.

Katie, I'm going to get you for this one!

The crazy part was this was Katie's type of activity. She loved being the center of attention with a bunch of kids and had a way of getting them to follow her easily. Those were Katie's special gifts, not Christy's.

A young girl ran screaming from the back of the bus and dove into the empty seat next to Christy as if her life depended on being protected from whatever was chasing her. Christy re-adjusted her legs to accommodate the flying banshee and asked in her sternest voice, "What is going on here?"

"Eeeeeeek!" the girl squealed, ducking and covering her head with her arms.

A cute kid with bright eyes and dark blond hair skidded down the aisle and slugged the girl in the back.

"Stop that right now!" Christy demanded.

"She took my candy," the boy hollered.

"Is that true?" Christy asked the girl, who was still bent over at the waist. Her matted hair hung over her face. The girl only giggled.

Christy asked again, "Did you take his candy?"

The girl kept giggling as Christy grabbed her by the shoulders and pulled her upright, revealing the stolen candy in her lap.

"Give it back," the boy spouted, grabbing the stash of candy bars and marching to his seat at the back of the bus.

As instantly as the seat beside Christy had filled, it now emptied. Giggling, the candy robber hopped up and returned to where her friends sat.

Christy felt a rush of relief when two college-age guys boarded the bus. With booming voices, they got the kids' attention and commanded them to settle down. To Christy's amazement, they did.

One of the guys announced the rules for the bus ride to camp. The other one asked them to bow their heads and close their eyes because he was going to pray for their trip to camp.

Christy added her own prayer at the end, *Lord, could you assign me a couple of extra guardian angels this week? I think I'm going to need them.*

CHAPTER FIVE

Camp Wildwood

Two hours later, when the bus rolled under a rustic wooden sign that read "Camp Wildwood," Christy felt an urge to jump bus and run for home. The word "rustic" would be a polite way to describe the camp. Christy's cabin was at the end of an uphill trail that made luggage-hauling miserable. Her fledglings followed her up the narrow, dusty trail, squealing and sobbing and making enough noise to scare off any wildlife for miles.

Somehow Christy knew the only wildlife she would experience this week would be in the form of pillow fights at three in the morning, frogs in her sleeping bag, and raids from the boys' cabins across the creek.

"Okay, girls," she called out as they stepped into their home sweet home. "I'm taking the bunk on the bottom here by the door. Everyone find a bunk. If you fight over who's on top, we'll swap positions halfway through the week."

The girls took to their nesting with lots of noise. Christy tried to let them solve their own problems while she smoothed out her sleeping bag. She found a note from her mom tucked inside.

May you have sweet dreams every night. Love, Mom.

Christy smiled and tucked it in her backpack. She pulled out her notebook just as two of the girls were about to exit.

"Whoa! Where are you going?" Christy said, stopping them. Suddenly she understood why, at the camp counselors meeting last night, they had made such a big deal about the counselors taking the bottom bunk by the door. It was the best spot to serve as a door guard.

"Out," the blond one answered.

"Not yet," Christy told her. "We have to have a cabin meeting first."

The girls acted as if she had just ordered them to eat raw Brussels sprouts and marched off to their bunks, pouting.

"Okay, everyone come sit on the floor. We're going to have a quick cabin meeting, and then you have free time until dinner."

"Can't we sit on our bunks?" asked a girl with ebony skin and big black eyes.

"Well, all right. As long as I can see all of you. Wait, I have an idea. Everyone sit on the top bunk. That way we can all see each other."

"I just made my bed," the girl across from Christy complained.

"I'd rather sit on the floor," another said.

"Can we eat in the cabin?" The request came from a plump blond who, from the chocolate smears around her lips, looked as though she had been eating ever since they left the church.

"No, it's one of the rules. The food attracts ants and other critters we don't want to invite into our cabin. Come on," Christy said, hoisting herself onto the empty top bunk above hers.

She realized if one of the bunks was empty that meant one of the girls hadn't made it to the cabin. Rather than leaving to find the lost sheep, she thought she had better go through her meeting as planned. Her list of campers would reveal who was missing, and then she could go after that person and at least know whom she was looking for.

"Quiet down, girls. You two in the back on the bottom bunk, could you join us please?"

It was the blond and her friend who had tried to escape earlier.

Christy looked over her list of names and said, "This will be a short meeting. I need to find out who's who. When I call out your name, please raise your hand."

"We're not back in school," the plump one said.

"What's your name?" the girl across from Christy asked.

"I'm Christy. Christy Miller."

"Do you have a boyfriend?" the blond in the back wanted to know.

"Well, actually," Christy hesitated, "let's talk about all that stuff later. First I need to find out your names." She started down the list. "Amy?"

"Present, Teach," mocked a girl across the room. She wore dangling earrings that looked a little too large for her small ears. Her coffee-colored hair was pulled up in a high ponytail, spilling over her head like a water fountain. With every movement, her hair and her earrings jiggled. She reminded Christy of a wild tropical bird. Even her "Present, Teach" sounded as though a "gawk" should be attached to the end.

"Jocelyn?"

The black girl raised her hand. "That's me." She looked as though she would be gorgeous once she grew into her strong features, like her eyes.

No eleven-year-old should be allowed to have eyelashes that long. She'll never have to spend a penny on mascara.

"Sara?"

"What?" the petite blond answered. She looked like a Skipper doll. Her wavy blond hair ran free all over her head, and her ginger eyes seemed to take in everything with a glance. Sara's T-shirt had the word "So?" printed on the front.

"Ruth," Christy called out.

"I like Ruthie better," the girl on the bunk across from her answered. "I hate my name. It sounds so blah."

"I like your name," Christy said. "It's the same as my grandmother's."

Some of the girls started to giggle, but tears welled up in Ruthie's eyes. "See what I mean? Your grandmother! Nobody my age is named Ruth."

She had a plain face, a long flat nose, and braces. Her skin was perfect, smooth, and without a freckle. Her light brown hair hung straight to the tip of her shoulders and was tucked behind her ear on the left side.

"Well, I like your name," Christy said, hoping to repair any damage she had done in the first fifteen minutes of their week together.

Christy called out the rest of the names. The only one who didn't answer was Jeanine Brown. She ran through the rules about camp boundaries, staying away from the guys' cabins, and not raiding cabins. Her confidence wasn't too high that any of the rules would be followed.

"Any questions?"

"Yeah," said Sara. "Do you have a boyfriend?"

"Sort of," Christy said. "And that's the best answer you're going to get from me. Now go enjoy your free time until dinner, and I'll look for all of you at the dining hall."

"Dining hall?" Jocelyn laughed. "Here it's a mess hall."

"Okay, fine. The mess hall. When the bell rings, go right to the mess hall. And wash your hands before you come in, okay?"

The girls were already elbowing their way out the door. Amy, the bird, called over her shoulder, "Yes, Teach."

Hopping down and tucking away her notebook, Christy kicked her big green duffel bag under her bed and headed out to find the missing Jeanine Brown. Halfway down the trail she heard the familiar squeal of the perky little thief who had collided with her on the bus on the way up. Christy went off the main trail and soon spotted the girl dashing from her hiding place behind a tree and running straight for Christy.

"Hide me!" she shrieked, grabbing Christy by the waist and using her as a shield.

"Give it back," hollered the boy whom the girl had harassed on the bus. He was galloping through the woods toward them.

"Never!" the girl shouted, giggling and pinching Christy's middle as she ducked behind her.

"She took my pocket knife," the exasperated boy said.

Christy jerked free of the girl's clutches, spun around, and in her firmest voice said, "Hand me the knife right now."

The girl sobered, pulled the deluxe Swiss army knife from the pocket of her jeans, and handed it to Christy with a repentant expression.

"What is your name, and who is your counselor?" Christy asked the boy.

"Nicholas. Jaeson is my counselor."

"Fine. At the counselors meeting tonight I'll give this to Jaeson, and he can give it back to you if he thinks you need it this week. As for you, who is your counselor?" she asked the sober-faced girl.

"I don't know."

"What cabin are you in?"

"I don't know."

"Where did you put your sleeping bag and luggage?"

"Down there, by the bus. I didn't know where to go."

"What's your name?" Christy asked, closing her eyes as she waited for the answer. She already knew what it would be.

"Jeanine Brown."

Nicholas took off into the woods, and Christy let out a sigh. "Come with me, Jeanine. I'm Christy Miller. I'm your counselor. Our cabin is at the top of the hill. Let's pick up your stuff."

"Oh, good!" Jeanine said joyfully. "I was hoping you would be my counselor."

Christy didn't feel she could return the compliment to her soon-to-be bunkmate. "Good," was all she managed to say. "Let's get going; it's almost dinnertime."

At least at dinner all her girls showed up. Amy wanted to sit by Christy at the large, round table, and Sara squabbled with Jocelyn over who would sit on the other side. It was nice, in a way, to be fought over. Then Christy reminded herself this was the first night and the first of many meals they would share. She hoped not every meal would be accompanied by so much hassle.

The food was good, better than she had expected. Amy dropped one of her dangling earrings in the bowl of applesauce as it was passed around, and Christy had to fish it out with the serving spoon. Before she could stop Amy, she had licked off the earring and poked it back in her ear.

"Do we have free time after dinner?" Jocelyn asked.

"Yes, but remember you have to stay in the camp boundaries. I'll be in a counselors meeting, so if you have any problems, wait for me outside the door of the lodge. We should be done in about an hour."

"Yes, Teach," Amy replied solemnly, her hair falling down on her face and touching the ends of her eyelashes.

The first question the camp dean, Bob Ferrill, asked in the counselors meeting was if their campers knew the counselors' names.

"Yes," Christy volunteered in the room of five of her peers. "Except one of them keeps calling me 'Teach.'"

"Don't worry," the dean said. "We've heard worse around here. Now we want all of you to meet each other. I prefer you call me Dean Ferrill rather than Bob or Mr. Ferrill."

The girl next to Christy was Jessica, and the other girl counselor was Diane. The guy counselors were Mike, Bob, and Jaeson. They each told where they lived and a little bit about themselves. Mike and Bob were two college guys from Christy's church. Jaeson was from the same church as Jessica and Diane.

Dean Ferrill explained that several of the campers were what he called "potentially high maintenance" because they were from difficult home situations. He explained that some of them would be acting as if they were younger than their age because of their emotional challenges.

"We're not going to label these kids because we want all of them to be treated equally, but we want you to know that you may have expectations of your campers that are higher than what some of them are capable of handling. Be patient. Love them all the same."

He went over the schedule for the evening, stressed the camp rules again, and then prayed. Christy thought his prayer was touching, especially when he prayed for each of the counselors and for the campers as if the salvation of each kid was the most important thing in his life. Christy knew she could survive the week with him on her side.

As the meeting broke up, Christy approached Jaeson. "Hi, I have something to give you. I forgot it back at my cabin. It's a pretty sophisticated pocket knife I confiscated from one of your boys. His name is Nicholas.''

''Yeah, Nick said one of the girls wouldn't leave him alone.''

Jaeson looked as though he was born to be a camp counselor. He had an athletic build and short black hair, with facial features that seemed chiseled out of stone. His sunglasses hung around his neck on a black foam strap, and on his wrist were half a dozen leather ''friendship bracelets'' the campers had learned to braid at craft time.

''Why don't you bring it to the meeting tonight? I'll keep it for him.''

''Thanks,'' Christy said.

She hurried up the trail to her cabin to grab her sweatshirt and the knife before the meeting started. When she opened the cabin door, three of the girls scampered like frightened mice.

''What are you guys doing?'' Christy asked, scanning the room for a clue. She spotted her make-up bag open on Amy's bed.

''Hey, what are you doing in my things?'' She looked at her bunk and saw her duffel bag was open with some of her clothes pulled halfway out.

The three culprits, Sara, Amy, and Jocelyn, stood frozen.

Sara spoke up. ''You said you were going to be in that meeting for about an hour. You weren't gone that long.''

''Wait a minute,'' Christy said firmly, feeling her temperature rising. ''The meeting has nothing to do with this. You got into my things without permission.'' She noticed that Amy appeared to have awfully pink cheeks and black smears around her eyes.

''Were you in my make-up, Amy?''

''Yes, Teach. But I was going to put it back.''

''That doesn't matter,'' Christy spouted, looking at the three of them sternly. "You *do not* get into other people's things! Do you understand me?"

The three solemnly nodded.

"Amy, go wash your face. Sara and Jocelyn, put my things back the way you found them. *Now!*"

The girls fled to obey the orders. Sara knelt to repack Christy's bag and started to sniffle.

"You're mean," Sara said under her breath. "I wish you weren't our counselor!"

Christy felt like saying the feeling was mutual when she noticed what Sara was wearing. "Is that my sweatshirt, by any chance?"

Sara pulled the sweatshirt off and threw it on the cabin floor. "I was only trying it on. I wasn't going to really wear it!"

Snatching it up, Christy shook it out and put it on. Then grabbing her backpack, she felt inside for the pocket knife, which was still there. The girls finished zipping up the bag full of now-crumpled clothes and rose to their feet. Sara was still crying, and Jocelyn's lip was lowered in a pout.

"We're sorry," Jocelyn said. "We won't do it again."

Something inside Christy told her to take both girls in her arms and hug them. Maybe these three were some of the ones who had special needs. But she was too upset at the moment. Instead Christy took two steps backward and ordered them to get their jackets and come to the evening meeting with her. Maybe the evening's message would straighten them out.

The girls obeyed, still sniffling. Amy met them at the door, her face scrubbed and her expression almost frightened.

"Get your jacket and come with us," Christy said firmly.

She marched them down the hill to the meeting, making them sit with her instead of with their friends. The singing was lively and fun, but Christy's three prisoners didn't join in. They sat quietly through the speaker's message.

Christy began to feel bad for coming down so hard on them. She knew they were still thinking about what had happened in the cabin and not paying attention to the message. As soon as the meeting was over, she told them they were free to go to the mess hall for the evening snack.

Just before the girls left the building, Jaeson came up to Christy and asked about the knife. She took her backpack off her shoulder to retrieve the knife and accidentally swung it too far, hitting Jaeson in the chest.

"Oh, I'm sorry! I didn't realize how heavy it was."

Jaeson appeared unaffected. He reached over and gently squeezed Christy's shoulder. "You're going to get a muscle spasm before the week is over if you keep carrying that around."

"I'll lighten the load tonight," she promised, noticing that the three girls had reappeared by her side. They were apparently curious as to what was going on between their counselor and this buff guy, who was touching her in public.

Christy handed Jaeson the pocket knife and said, "I told Nick you would decide whether to give it back to him."

"No problem," Jaeson said. "Thanks for catching it for me."

"Can I try on your sunglasses?" Sara asked, looking up at Jaeson, her ginger eyes bright with admiration.

"Maybe tomorrow," he said kindly. "You'd better run over to the mess hall if you want to get any cookies before the guys scarf them all."

"Are you coming?" Sara asked.

"Sure, we'll go with you," Jaeson said. "Come on, Christy. They always have peanut butter cookies on Sunday nights. They're the best."

"You've done this before, I take it," Christy said as they were escorted across camp by three sets of big ears.

"This is my third year. I started last week, and I'm staying until the end of July. How about you?"

"This is my first time as a counselor. I'm not sure I'm going to be very good at this," she admitted, still feeling bad for the way she had treated the girls.

"Oh, you're the best counselor we've ever had, isn't she?" Sara asked the other two girls. "And she's pretty too, isn't she, Jaeson?"

Christy felt her cheeks warming. How could these little girls change their opinion of her so instantly?

Before Jaeson could answer, Amy popped in with, "And if there's anything she needs to learn about camp, you can teach her. 'Cuz she's our Teach, so you can teach her. Get it?"

By then, thankfully, they had arrived at the mess hall, and Jaeson graciously said, "If I can help you out in any way, let me know. I'm sure you'll have a great week."

"Oh, she will, won't you, Teach?" Amy answered enthusiastically before running off with the other girls in a fit of giggles.

That night it took two hours for the girls to settle down. Even then, Christy worried that one of them might fake being asleep and would sneak out the minute she dozed off. She lay half awake, half asleep, listening for rustling in the silence.

After some time, she checked her alarm clock with her flashlight: 1:25.

I'm never going to wake up at six! And this is only the first night.

The second night didn't go much better. The day was packed with activities for the campers. Christy thought for sure with all the swimming, horseback riding, and archery, combined with last night's late hours, the girls would willingly tumble into bed.

No, they wanted to talk. About boys.

"You girls are only going into the fifth grade. You're too young to be so interested in boys," Christy said from her bunk once she had gotten them all in bed and the lights out.

"People mature faster now," Sara informed her. "We're much more grown-up than we were last year. When did you first start to like guys?"

Christy had to think back. She remembered going to summer camp with her best friend, Paula, right before they went into seventh grade. When she thought about it, she and Paula did spend most of that week trying to get the boys' attention.

"It doesn't matter," Christy said. "The point is, there's lots more to do at camp than occupy yourselves with guys. Besides, none of them seems to be very interested in you girls yet. You see, girls mature more quickly than boys."

"We know all that, Teach," Amy said from her bunk across the dark cabin. "Tell us stuff we don't know."

"Stuff you don't know?" Christy asked.

"Yeah, like what it's like to be kissed by your boyfriend," Sara said.

"She said she only 'sort of' had a boyfriend," Amy interjected. "I think Jaeson wants to be your boyfriend."

All the girls joined in a noisy chorus of agreement and approval.

"Hush," Christy said. "We have to be quiet or Dean Ferrill will come up like he did last night and tell us to settle down. I don't want to get in trouble again."

"Don't you think he's cute?" Jocelyn said in a loud whisper.

"Who?" Christy said, playing it cool, "Dean Ferrill? Sure, I suppose he's cute, for a man who's old enough to be my father."

"No, not him, Jaeson."

"You know what, girls?" Christy said sternly. "It's too late to have a discussion like this. I want you all to quiet down and go to sleep."

A round of complaints followed.

"I mean it!" Christy said gruffly. "All of you settle down right now."

Just then there was a loud knock on their cabin door. Dean Ferrill's voice boomed out. "Is everything okay, Christy?"

"Yes," Christy answered. "The girls were just going to sleep, weren't you girls?"

Someone faked loud snoring, and another girl said, "Hey, stop knocking on our door! We're trying to sleep in here."

"Good night, ladies," the dean said firmly. "I don't want to have to come back up here to check on you again."

"You won't have to," Christy promised. "We're going to sleep now."

The girls remained quiet as they listened to Dean Ferrill walk away from their cabin.

All of a sudden, into the stillness, Sara called out, "Hey, Dean Ferrill, Christy thinks you're cute, for an old guy!"

CHAPTER SIX

What You Can Never Do

"How are you doing, Christy?" Dean Ferrill asked the next morning at the counselors meeting.

"Pretty good. I apologize for Sara's comment last night."

"Don't worry about it. How do the girls seem to be responding spiritually?"

"Not much, I'd say. I could use some pointers on what I should be doing."

"What are your plans for cabin devos?" Jessica asked. She carried herself like a model, with straight posture and gentle movements. She had excelled during the swimming competition the day before.

Her caramel-colored hair was back in a ponytail today, and her delicate face looked as though she followed a strict skin-care program. Without a touch of make-up she looked beautiful.

"Cabin devos?" Christy asked.

"Devotions. What are you doing with the girls at night before you go to bed?"

"Yelling at them," Christy answered, half joking, half serious.

"Devotions really help to calm them down, and I think you'll get the most open responses from them then," Jessica said.

"Would you like to get together during free time this afternoon? I could give you some ideas."

"Great! I'd appreciate that."

Christy thought she noticed Jaeson smiling at her. She wondered if it was because he was thinking she was inexperienced or if he was being nice. The meeting again ended with a wonderful prayer time for the campers. Christy felt certain something of eternal value would have to break through with her girls soon, the way everyone was praying.

That morning at recreation, Christy's girls went up against Jaeson's boys at archery. Christy didn't look forward to the competition. She hadn't shot a bow and arrow since she was in junior high. Thankfully her girls had come to expect her to be the expert in everything, and right now she appreciated all the votes of confidence she could get from them.

The girls all lined up, facing the stacks of hay with the target tacked to the center. Christy picked up a bow and showed her girls how to hold it and aim for the target. She let the arrow fly. It whooshed a grand total of about three feet and landed uncomfortably close to Jaeson's foot.

The campers broke into laughter as the red-faced Christy made her way to the boys' side to retrieve her wayward arrow.

"Sorry," she muttered to Jaeson. "I don't know what went wrong."

"You had your elbow down. Hold it up flat like this," Jaeson said, demonstrating with the bow in his hand.

Christy tried to imitate his stance and elbow position. It didn't feel right. "Like this? Or higher?" she asked.

"May I?" Jaeson asked, putting down his bow and stepping over next to Christy. He put his muscular arm around her shoulders and placed his hand on top of hers. "Pull back like this," he instructed. "Keep your elbow up. Do you feel that?"

Christy was starting to feel something, all right. She felt the eyes of her campers drinking in the scene before them. She knew she would never convince them that he was only helping her.

"Now try," Jaeson said, stepping back.

Christy let go of the taut string, and the arrow zinged through the air, hitting the white part of the circle.

"All right! Good job!" Jaeson praised. "You guys all see that?"

A couple of the older boys said, "Yeah, we saw it, Jaeson. You sure you don't want us to leave so you two can be alone?"

Jaeson ignored the comment. He put his arm around the shoulders of the first boy in line and demonstrated the correct position the same way he had with Christy.

She approached her flock of twittering birdies with a serious expression. "Who's first?"

The girls had giddy expressions in their eyes as they whispered among themselves.

"Sara," Christy called, "you try it first."

Christy wrapped her arm around Sara and imitated Jaeson's correct archery stance. She hoped the girls would think this was the way everyone was taught how to shoot an arrow, with your arm around them.

Ignoring all the "Cupid" comments, Christy patiently showed each girl how to shoot. She was amazed at how readily the girls responded as she put her arm around them. They seemed eager to please her, and she began to see them in a different light. Not as brats, but as babies away from home and needing a big hug.

When their time was almost up, Christy glanced over at the boys and saw Jaeson watching her. He smiled and gave her a thumbs-up sign.

She felt as if, during the last few days, she had been building up a reservoir of wonder about Jaeson. She wondered if he liked her. She wondered if he were looking at her across the mess hall. She wondered if he were going to be at the pool during free time.

With Jaeson's thumbs-up, the reservoir of wonder overflowed, flooding her with thoughts of Jaeson, Jaeson, Jaeson.

At lunch she looked for where he was sitting before she chose her table. The rule was only one counselor at each table. She thought if she spotted him right away, she could sit at the table next to his so their chairs would be back to back. Her plan worked. There was an empty table next to his and an empty chair behind him. She slid in quietly, as if she didn't notice he was there.

"Hi," Jaeson said. "Did you see the final score on the archery practice?"

"No, I didn't. How did we do?"

"Your girls beat my guys by ten points."

"You're kidding! I never would have guessed it," Christy said, smiling. "Thanks for all your help."

"Anytime," Jaeson said, smiling back.

Just then the mess hall doors opened, and the campers were let in. They ran like escaping guinea pigs, not sure where they were going but feverish about being the first one to get there. Christy's girls filled in at her table in record time and took turns poking each other with their elbows.

Jessica came over to Christy's table with two adoring campers holding on to each arm. "Where do you want to meet after lunch?" Jessica asked above the roar.

Christy shrugged, looking to Jessica for a suggestion.

"How about the lodge?"

Christy nodded, and Jessica surrendered to the persuasion of her two-arm fan club.

When Christy went to meet Jessica in the lodge as arranged, she kept checking over her shoulder to see if Jaeson were following her. He seemed to be headed in the direction of the craft barn. Maybe she should go over after her meeting with Jessica—to check on any of her girls that might be there, of course.

"First," Jessica said when they had seated themselves on the old couch, "I'm not trying to tell you how to relate to your girls. I know you're doing a great job. I didn't want you to think I was trying to step in this morning and tell you what to do."

"I didn't think that at all. I need all the help I can get!"

For half an hour Jessica made some good suggestions about how to put a devotion together and what worked best for her last year when she was a counselor for the first time.

"It's actually easier this year with the group I have. They're the youngest batch, the ones just going into fourth grade. Some of them are having a hard time because this is the first time they've been away from home on their own. And they're not real good about their hygiene without being reminded. But they're not real boy-crazy yet. At least not all of them."

"They sure like you," Christy said.

"Well, I think I'm learning from some of the mistakes I made last summer. I didn't realize until after camp what I did wrong, and I'm trying to do it differently this year."

"Can I ask what it was?" Christy asked cautiously. Jessica seemed so approachable, she thought it would be okay to ask such a personal question.

"Christy, I'll tell you, there is one thing you can never do."

Just then Christy's little boy-chaser, Jeanine, burst through the lodge's door, clutching a baseball cap in her fist. With ear-shattering squeals, she ran behind the couch and pleaded, "Don't let him get me!"

Outside the door, Nick obeyed the "No Campers" sign and stayed outside, peering in for a glimpse of Jeanine.

"That's it!" Christy shouted, jumping up and demanding the cap from Jeanine. "This has gone on too long. Give me the cap. Now leave the poor kid alone and don't take anything else of his. Do you understand me?"

Jeanine handed over the cap with the look of a scolded puppy. "I'm sorry," she said in a small voice.

Christy stomped over to the door and delivered the cap to Nick, who looked slightly annoyed. Two of his friends joined him and stood on either side for moral support.

"Will you tell her to stop it?" Nick asked Christy.

"You know what, Nicholas, it's only a game if both of you play. If you stop playing, it won't be fun to her anymore, and I guarantee she'll stop."

"Not likely," one of Nick's bodyguards mumbled.

Nick slipped the cap back on his head, and the three of them trudged off to the baseball field. Christy watched them go and almost laughed aloud. They were miniature versions of Todd, Doug, and Rick.

Elephants, monkeys, and snakes. Oh, my.

When Christy turned around, she discovered Jeanine had taken her place next to Jessica on the couch. Jessica, the experienced counselor, was stroking the young girl's hair out of her face and speaking to her softly. Jeanine drank in every word.

"Okay, I'll try it," Jeanine said, hopping up and giving Jessica a look she never would have given to Christy. A look of true admiration and appreciation. Then she rushed out of the lodge.

"What did you tell her?" Christy asked, retrieving her seat on the couch.

"I told her that instead of taking things away from Nick,

maybe she should try giving something to him to get his attention. She's off to make a friendship bracelet at the craft center."

"That was brilliant. How did you think of that?"

"It's what I was about to tell you before she burst in here. The one thing you can never do is love too much."

"Never love too much?" Christy repeated.

"When I left camp last year, I realized I had done a lot of the 'right' things as a counselor, but I hadn't loved the girls in my cabin as much as I could have. Do you know what I mean?"

Christy flashed back to when she had caught the girls going through her clothes. Yes, she did know what Jessica meant.

"You see," Jessica said, "you can't argue with love. When this week is over, what will the girls remember? The squabbles? The team races on the last day? What the speaker said?"

"I'm sure they'll remember some of that," Christy said. "I remember some of that from my days as a camper."

"But what do you remember the most?" Jessica asked. "Not just about camp, but about your whole life? I think we remember the people who loved us."

Christy took Jessica's advice to heart. She knew her new friend was right. Eagerly making her way to the craft barn after their meeting, Christy wondered how that advice might apply to Jaeson. What would he remember about her when camp was over?

More and more thoughts collided in her head as if all her emotions had gathered and were holding court in her brain. She was the one on trial. The prosecuting attorney's voice said she was silly and immature to chase after a guy at summer camp when she had Todd waiting for her at home. Another emotion stepped up as her defense witness and claimed she had the right to build relationships with any guy she wanted to, and this was all part of camp.

Just as she was about to enter the craft barn, Christy imagined all the girls in her cabin as the jury. Their squeaky voices were raised in a loud "Not guilty" inside her head. She felt free to take that step into the craft barn and see what happened next.

She noticed Jaeson right away. He looked up and saw her at the same time.

"Christy," he greeted her, "just the person I wanted to see. Can you help these girls with their bracelets? I'm supposed to meet my guys at the pool in five minutes."

Sara, Amy, and Jocelyn beamed their approval at her and started to talk all at once. Christy stepped over to the side of the table where the three of them were nearly finished braiding their friendship bracelets.

"Can you tie mine?" Sara asked. "I'm all done. Do you like it? Does it look right?"

"Yes, it's very nice," Christy said, tying the two leather straps around Sara's thin wrist. "You did a nice job."

Jaeson squeezed Christy's shoulder and said, "Thanks a million for helping me out here. I'll see you later. At the pool, maybe?"

"Sure, we'll come to the pool," Amy answered for her. "Won't we, Teach? We're really done, aren't we, you guys?"

"I'll see you," Jaeson called over his shoulder as he took off for the pool.

The minute Jaeson was out the door, Sara smiled at Christy and said, "Jaeson asked if you had a boyfriend, and we told him 'no' because you never told us if you really had one or not. We told him you liked him, and he said he liked you."

The three girls gathered around Christy with their eyes twinkling.

"So? Do you like him?" Amy asked.

Christy wasn't sure how much of all this she should believe. She decided a strong, direct answer might work best. "I think Jaeson is a really nice guy. He's a strong Christian, and that's a very important quality to look for in a guy."

"We knew it!" Sara squealed. "We knew you liked him! Come on. Let's go to the pool."

Jocelyn and Amy held out their arms for Christy to tie their bracelets and then joined Sara, racing up the hill to their cabin to put on their bathing suits.

Christy realized Jeanine must have gotten sidetracked because she wasn't busily making her bracelet for Nick. Either that or she had been so enthusiastic she had already finished it and rushed off to present it to her "boyfriend."

Taking a few minutes to close up the craft barn, Christy headed up the hill. The girls met her halfway, already suited and with towels under their arms.

"We'll see you there!" they shouted and scampered on down the hill to the pool.

When Christy met them a short time later, they were having a water war with Jaeson and his guys. She wasn't sure she wanted to step into the middle of their combat. To her relief, the lifeguard blew his whistle and said they were getting too rowdy and had to get out of the pool. She put down her towel on the warm cement.

Her three little drowned rats were the first ones out, complaining and arguing about how the boys weren't playing fair. They wrapped themselves in their towels and sat down right next to Christy, hurling rude comments at the boys.

Jaeson planted himself in the middle of his guys and tried to calm them down. He glanced over at Christy, smiled, and shrugged as if to say, "What am I supposed to do with these clowns?"

Christy smiled back.

"He likes you," Sara said, lifting Christy's left hand and pressing down on Christy's fingernails. "Are these real? I mean, are they yours?"

"Yes, they're mine and they're real."

"They're so long!" Sara exclaimed as Amy and Jocelyn crowded in to feel Christy's nails.

"Not really," Christy said.

"They're longer than mine," Amy said. "How do you make them grow?"

"First of all, try to stop biting them," Christy suggested.

"I bite mine all the time," Jocelyn confessed.

The girls continued to compare their nails with Christy's and each other's. Christy peered over their heads and noticed Jaeson talking with the lifeguard. The lifeguard blew his whistle, signaling for everyone in the pool to stop where they were.

"We're going to put up the volleyball net in the shallow end," the lifeguard announced. "Everyone who wants to play volleyball go in the shallow end. Everyone else stay in the deep end."

Apparently volleyball was Jaeson's idea, because he had already pulled the net from the storage cupboard, and his boys were helping him to set it up.

"I don't want to play with them," Amy said. "They always cheat. We'll stay here with you."

Christy's fan club positioned their towels closer to her, overlapping her towel and dripping all over her.

"You want to play?" Jaeson called out to Christy from the shallow end as soon as he had the net in place.

"No!" Sara answered, grabbing Christy by the arm.

The other girls followed her lead. "She's staying here with us."

Christy felt a strong urge to break free from these wet, clinging urchins, but Jessica's advice prompted her to stay. This was a chance for her to show these girls she loved them. Besides, she wasn't much of a volleyball player on land. She had a feeling the water wouldn't improve her skills.

Now it was Christy's turn to smile and shrug back at Jaeson. He gave her one of his thumbs-up signs and tossed the ball into the water. For the rest of free time, Christy hung around the pool, watching Jaeson, talking to her girls, and wondering if Jaeson would come over and talk to her. He never did, but he looked at her a lot.

At dinner, Christy arrived in the mess hall before Jaeson and took a seat at an empty table, watching the door. He soon came in and headed right for Christy.

"There you are," he said, taking the seat that backed up to hers at the next table. "Your girls told me you didn't have one of these yet."

Jaeson used his teeth to remove one of the leather friendship bracelets from his wrist and offered it to Christy. "You're not an official Camp Wildwood counselor unless you have one of these."

"Thanks," Christy said, holding out her left wrist for Jaeson to tie on the bracelet. Her "Forever" ID bracelet circled her right wrist, and she didn't think the two bracelets mixed.

While Jaeson tied the thin leather straps, the doors opened and the campers ran in. Christy's girls flocked to her table in time to see him finish tying on the bracelet and give Christy a big smile, which she returned. That's all it took for them to all start whispering about how Jaeson and Christy were now going together.

The eager group of matchmakers made sure that Christy sat near Jaeson in the evening meeting and that they walked to the mess hall together for evening snack.

Christy had to admit it was fun playing the role of heroine. Six of her girls had now permanently attached themselves to her and led her by the arms wherever they wanted her to go, telling her how pretty she looked or how much Jaeson liked her.

Jaeson seemed to enjoy being a hero too. Christy could tell he had been through this kind of treatment many times before because of all his years as a counselor. She knew it must be like this for him every week of camp. She also figured she was one in a long line of girl counselors who were destined to be Jaeson's girlfriend for the week.

It didn't matter. Christy was having too much fun to think of why this game should end.

The next morning she found it hard to wake up. It was Wednesday, halfway through the week. They had been warned in a counselors meeting that this was when it would all begin to catch up with them.

The girls seemed to have no problem bouncing out of bed, though. Christy pulled her sleeping bag over her head and tried to catch a few more Z's.

"Aren't you going to take a shower?" Sara asked, rocking Christy by the shoulder. "You always get up and take a shower."

"Just let me sleep five more minutes," Christy pleaded. "Five more minutes."

"But it's almost 6:30," one of the girls said. "You have to get to the mess hall before seven so you can get a table next to Jaeson's."

"Oh, I do, do I?" Christy asked, throwing back the sleeping bag and facing seven curious faces peering at her.

"Yes," they all agreed. "He really likes you, and he would be mad at you if you didn't get there in time."

"Oh, he would, would he?" Christy pulled her legs from her snug cocoon and forced them into the cool morning air and onto the cluttered wood floor.

"You guys, this place is a mess," Christy scolded. "We only received five points yesterday for cabin cleanup. Today I want us to get all ten points. That means everyone has to pick up her junk and put it away."

"Here, wear this," Amy said, pulling a T-shirt from Christy's bag, laying it on her sleeping bag, and smoothing out the wrinkles with her hand.

"And your jeans shorts," Jocelyn advised.

"Okay, okay! You girls get yourselves dressed. And don't forget to pick up all your junk." Christy was beginning to dislike this part of the day when she couldn't go to the bathroom or wash her face without bracing herself against the morning chill on the hike to the rest rooms. Throwing on her clothes and grabbing her towel and make-up bag, she headed out the door.

"We'll go with you," four of the girls echoed. "Wait for us."

Christy stood outside the cabin door, shivering and waiting for her entourage to get its act together. The girls joined her, all chattering brightly as they trudged through the dirt.

When Christy arrived in the bathroom, Jessica was already there with her fan club. She looked fresh and pretty and ready to start the day.

"How do you do that?"

"What?"

"How do you manage to look so awake? I'm exhausted."

"We got to bed on time last night, finally," Jessica said. "I cut my devos short. How did yours work out last night?"

Christy plunged her washcloth into the cold water and washed her face as quickly as she could. "Brrr!" she said, patting dry with her musty-smelling towel. "Devos went well, I think."

The campers were all scurrying around the bathroom. A few huddled around the sink next to Jessica and Christy and imitated the older girls' wake-up routine by splashing cold water on their faces and responding with the same "Brrr!"

"They were great!" Jocelyn answered for Christy. "We talked all night."

"I tried your idea of getting acquainted by each girl telling about her family. We went too long, but they all had lots to say. I think I know them a lot better now."

"And she likes us more, too," Amy added. "Don't you, Teach?"

Jessica and Christy exchanged smiles.

"You can never love too much," Jessica whispered in Christy's ear. Then gathering her things, she said, "You're doing a great job, Christy. I'll see you at breakfast."

Christy felt warmed inside and encouraged. Maybe she was going to make it through this week after all.

CHAPTER SEVEN

Tippy Canoe

Wednesday zoomed by with the usual routine of counselors meeting, morning Bible study, and the whole afternoon free. Christy planned to spend the afternoon at the pool with her girls since Jaeson said he was going to be there. But when she went up to the cabin to put on her bathing suit, she found Ruthie on her bunk bed, crying.

Christy sat on the edge of Ruthie's bed, ducking her head to fit under the top bunk. She placed her hand on Ruthie's back and slowly rubbed it. "Are you okay?"

Ruthie's sobbing slowed to a sniffle. "Nobody here likes me."

"Yes, they do. Everyone likes you. I like you very much," Christy said.

"Everybody has her own friends here. I don't have anybody. Nobody asked me to go with them. They all took off without me."

Christy kept rubbing Ruthie's back and stroked her light brown hair back from her peaches-and-cream face. "I'm sorry," was all Christy said.

She thought of plenty of advice to give Ruthie about how she should be the friendly one who pursues the other girls and how it wouldn't do any good to lie here feeling sorry for herself when there was so much outside for her to do. But Christy remembered the times she had felt left out, lonely, and sad. It had always helped to throw herself on her bed and have a good cry.

What she didn't like was when her mom had come in and told her how she should act or what she should be feeling. Christy always wished her mother would just let her cry and feel sad with her for a few minutes.

Christy sat silently rubbing Ruthie's back as she finished getting out all her tears. Eventually the only sound was a few sniffs from Ruthie into her damp pillow.

"Here," Christy said, reaching over to her backpack on the floor and pulling out a packet of tissues. "Try one of these instead of your pillowcase. You're going to have to sleep on that thing tonight, you know."

Ruthie accepted the tissue and blew her nose. "You probably think I'm acting like a baby."

"Not at all," Christy said, handing her another tissue. "I think you're a lovely young girl turning into a beautiful young woman."

The girl honked her nose loudly as she blew. "Sorry," she said, repressing a giggle at how loud her nose sounded.

"That's okay," Christy said. "You feel better?"

Ruthie nodded and offered a smile.

"Good. Now what do you want to do this afternoon? You and I can do it together."

"I wanted to go out in a canoe, but nobody else wanted to go with me."

"I'll go with you," Christy said.

"Are you sure?" Ruthie asked. "Wouldn't you rather be with Jaeson?"

"No, I'd rather be with you."

Ruthie sprang from the bed, her hope renewed, and led the way to the door. Christy followed, feeling pleased with Ruthie's comeback. On the trail to the lake, Ruthie slipped her hand into Christy's and gave it a squeeze. Christy squeezed back.

"How did you get so good at knowing what to do when a girl is crying?"

"I happen to be the pity-party expert," Christy said. "When I was your age I used to cry about stuff all the time."

"And you don't cry anymore?"

"Sure, I still cry, but not as much. I still have some of the same feelings that used to send me to my pillow when I was younger, but they don't make me cry as much anymore."

Ruthie let go of Christy's hand and skittered a few feet into the woods, where she picked a small yellow wildflower and brought it back to Christy.

"Thank you, Ruthie," Christy said, slipping the flower behind her right ear. "And I really do like your name. There was a Ruth in the Bible, you know. There's a whole book written about her because she was such a loyal friend. That's how I'll always re-member you: as Ruthie, my loyal friend."

Ruthie flashed a rare, full smile, revealing her mouthful of sil-ver braces. She looked like a different girl from the sullen one who had told Christy she hated the name Ruth.

They walked through the clearing onto the gravel beach by the lake. Ruthie was the first to notice that two of the other girls from their cabin, Sara and Jeanine, were there.

Christy knew if Jeanine was here Nick probably was not far away. Sure enough, Christy spotted Nick and his two friends at the boat shack, apparently getting a canoe.

"Why don't you ask those two girls if they'd like to join us on our canoe ride?" Christy suggested to Ruthie. "I have a strong feeling at least one of them would like to."

Ruthie ran off to invite Jeanine and Sara while Christy headed for the boat shack. Not until she was in front of the shack did she notice Jaeson was the one behind the window passing out life vests.

"Christy, just the person I wanted to see. How do you feel about taking these guys for a canoe ride? I told Mike I'd fill in for him here until four."

"She's taking us out," Jeanine answered, stepping up to the window with Ruthie and Sara.

"We could take one of the guys," Jeanine added, flashing a grin at Nick.

"Nope," Jaeson said. "Only four to a canoe."

Jaeson looked at his watch and then back at Nick and his two friends. "I probably shouldn't do this," he said, "but you guys have gone out before, and you pretty much know what you're doing. I'll let you three go by yourselves. Christy, can you keep an eye on them and try to stay close to them out on the lake in case of any accidents?"

"Sure, that's fine," Christy said.

"And I'll be right here watching you guys," Jaeson added, handing out the life preservers. He caught Christy's wrist when she reached for her preserver and gave it a squeeze. "Thanks. You're a honey."

Christy's campers heard him say it, and they huddled close to her as they walked over to the canoes.

"He likes you!" Jeanine declared nice and loud.

"Shhhh," Christy said. Then bending close to Jeanine, she asked, "How's it going with you and Nick?"

"Okay, I think. He hasn't hit me yet today."

"And you haven't taken any more of his things, have you?"

"No. I gave him a bracelet like Jessica said, but he's not wearing it."

"That's okay." Christy gave her a little squeeze around her plump orange life vest. "I'm proud of the way you're acting."

Jeanine beamed.

It took Christy's troop longer to launch their boat than the boys. They suddenly had four captains and no mates. Jaeson came over and helped by giving their canoe a good swift push. Christy sat at the front with a paddle in her hand, Ruthie took the middle bench, and Jeanine and Sara insisted on sharing the back seat, each with a paddle in the water.

"Make sure you paddle in the same direction," Jaeson called out as they began to bob on the calm lake.

"Farewell!" Sara cried out dramatically, standing up and turning to wave good-bye to Jaeson.

"Sit down!" they all yelled at her as the canoe began to tip.

"Okay, listen," Christy called over her shoulder. "All of you follow my lead. If my paddle is in the water on this side, then you put your paddle in on this side. And the same over here." She demonstrated for them, hoping none of them would guess that she hadn't been in a canoe since she was their age. Even then, it was with her Uncle Tom in Minnesota, and he had done all the paddling.

The crew followed orders, and everything seemed smooth. No problem.

"Let's catch up with the boys," Jeanine said, eagerly paddling on her side. The canoe swerved to the left toward the shore.

"We have to paddle all together," Christy said. "Remember what I said? Follow my lead."

She dug her paddle into the water for three strong strokes on the left side of the canoe to straighten them out and at least point them in the boys' direction. Christy switched her paddle to the right side, but apparently the girls weren't watching. Sara and Ruthie kept paddling on the left. It seemed they were getting no-where.

Christy barked out more instructions. The canoe gently drifted toward the middle of the lake, no thanks to their efforts.

"Look at the ducks!" Sara said. "They're coming right up to the canoe. Let's sit here and watch them."

"No, we need to catch up with the boys," Jeanine objected. "Remember what Jaeson said. We have to stay with them, and they're headed for the other side of the lake."

"What's over there?" Christy asked.

"That's where they have the counselor hunt on the last full day," Sara explained. "All the counselors row over in canoes and hide, and then we run around the edge of the lake to find them. Whoever finds their counselor first has to get their counselor's sash and run all the way back to the boat shack."

"But the counselors get to try to beat them," Jeanine added. "They come back in their canoes and have to plant their flags by the boat house."

"Sounds like a lot of fun," Christy said.

"Whoever loses has to serve the food at the banquet on the last night. We have team captains, and if the campers lose, they serve the counselors, who all sit together at one table."

"And if the counselors lose?" Christy asked.

"Then they have to serve all the tables."

"Well, I hope we win. I wouldn't mind having dinner served to me," Christy said. "Paddle on the right, girls. We're starting to drift too far."

They worked their way across the lake, improving as they

went, until they almost caught up with the boys. Christy could feel strange muscle twinges in her upper arms. She never would have guessed paddling was such hard work or that this small lake was so far across.

"How are you guys doing?" Christy called out when they were within a few yards of the guys' canoe.

"We're fishing," Nick said. He pulled his stick out of the water and revealed a brown string attached to it with a wiggly worm at the end. Christy thought their Tom Sawyer fishing pole looked quite clever.

"Ewww!" Sara said. "That's a worm."

"Duh," said one of the boys.

"I hate worms," Sara said.

Nick dangled the fishing pole over toward the girls' canoe so Sara could look at the worm close up. It came within a few feet of her face, and she screamed.

"Hey," Jeanine yelled when she looked closely at the brown string attached to the stick, "that's the friendship bracelet I made for you!"

"Turned out to be good for something," Nick said, laughing.

"I want it back!" Jeanine yelled. "I worked hard on that. You're not supposed to use it for a fishing line!"

Jeanine stood up and lunged for the line, which Nick jerked away. Before Christy knew what was happening, Jeanine toppled from the canoe and into the lake.

"Jeanine!" Christy screamed, turning around and trying to steady the topsy-turvy canoe. Sara stood and tried to reach for the soaked Jeanine.

Ruthie leaned back to compensate for Sara's weight being thrown to one side, but it was too much of a compensation. The canoe tottered to the left, dumping Ruthie into the lake and then to the right, dumping Sara in after Jeanine.

"Girls!" Christy called out futilely. The canoe rocked back and forth, and Christy tried to steady it as the three drowned rats, buoyed up by their life vests, each tried to pull themselves into the canoe on opposite sides. The girls were laughing and didn't seem to mind the dunking a bit.

"Wait!" Christy cried. "Stop! This isn't working. We're so close to shore, why don't you swim in, and I'll pick you up there?"

The girls, still laughing, willingly dog-paddled the short distance to shore and waited there for Christy, dripping wet and shivering.

The boys were laughing so hard they didn't hear Christy tell them to stay put while she went for the girls. They must have decided their best course of action was to get as far away from the girls as they could, since they knew retaliation would be on the girls' minds. The boys took off, paddling full speed back to the boat shack, leaving Christy to manage the rescue landing by herself.

The girls helped pull their canoe into shore and stiffly tried to get in. That's when the laughing stopped and the complaining began.

"They made us fall in," Jeanine sobbed. "I'm going to get back at them."

"I'm cold," Sara complained. "Didn't you bring a towel?"

"It's back on the other side," Christy said. "Once we get over there you can use it."

"But it's so far," Ruthie moaned. "We're going to freeze to death."

"It's not that cold," Christy said. "Try sitting in the bottom of the canoe. You'll keep out of the wind better that way."

"But there's water in the bottom," Sara said.

"That's okay," Christy coaxed them. "You're already wet. It won't hurt you."

The girls wedged themselves into the hull of the canoe and crossed their arms in front of them around their bloated vests, trying to keep warm. Christy, at the helm, tried her best to maneuver the canoe across the lake. It seemed impossible to move the canoe in the direction she wanted it to go. Without anyone paddling at the rear, the canoe floundered through the water, more motivated by the wind and waves than by Christy's determined efforts with the paddle. She was definitely doing this the hard way.

Her complaining crew kept giving her advice about which side she should be paddling on and why she was doing it all wrong. Christy endured the remarks for ten minutes and then lost it. "Would one of you like to try this?" she barked. "It's not exactly easy."

"I'll help you," Ruthie offered. She rose to sit on the middle seat and stuck a paddle into the water on the same side as Christy's. Together they plunged the canoe through the water and made some headway.

Ten minutes later they reached the shore. By then the girls were mostly dried out. The boys had landed a good fifteen minutes earlier and had long since disappeared.

Jaeson met them at the shore, wading waist deep in the water to help bring in their canoe. He lifted each of the girls from their floating prison and offered his hand to Christy so she could step out onto the gravel. She felt like an incompetent counselor, having dumped her girls and having lost track of the boys. If she had fallen in herself, she might have felt better at this moment. At least she could have been another victim and not the responsible person.

Jaeson held onto her hand and drew her close. In a low voice he said, "Would you be interested in a free canoe lesson?"

A smile returned to Christy's face. "Why?" she teased. "You think I need one?"

"It's up to you," Jaeson said. "I thought you might want a little edge on the campers for the counselor hunt on Friday."

"Okay, you talked me into it," Christy said. "You say when, and I'll be there."

"I'll let you know tonight at dinner," Jaeson said, giving her hand a squeeze before letting it go.

At dinner, Jaeson and Christy sat back to back in what had become their usual spots at the tables. During the meal Jaeson leaned back four times to make comments in Christy's ear. It was hard to hear him above the roar of the campers. But it didn't really matter what he said. Just the attention was fun.

She did notice when dinner was over that he hadn't mentioned a time for the promised canoe lesson. Maybe he had forgotten. Christy tried not to feel discouraged. After all, this was only Wednesday, and they had the whole next day to practice, since the race was on Friday.

"Come play softball with us," her girls urged, pulling her by the arms from the mess hall. "We have to hurry! We only have a half-hour free before the evening meeting starts."

Christy let the girls lead her out to the baseball field where some of the campers had already started up a game. When they saw her coming, they all insisted she be the pitcher. She was good at hitting the ball, but she wasn't too confident her pitching would win any awards.

Taking her place on the mound and winding up, she let the softball fly over home plate. Thump! One of the girls from Jessica's cabin hit the ball, and it sailed to center field. Her teammates cheered, and the girl took a playful bow when she made it safely to first base.

Another wind up, and the next girl made contact with the first ball Christy pitched. Same with the next hitter; the bases were loaded. A timid, skinny fifth-grader stepped up to the plate next, and Christy threw three of the gentlest, slowest balls she could throw. The girl swung at all three and missed.

"One more pitch," a deep voice called out from the side of the field. It was Jaeson. He stepped up behind the discouraged little hitter, wrapped his arms around her, and showed her how to hold the bat the right way.

"Okay, Christy," Jaeson called out, his arms still around the batter. "Give us your best shot."

Christy pretended to be spitting on her hands and sending signals to the catcher.

"Come on, pitcher," Jaeson yelled, "let us have it!"

With a dramatic windup, Christy let the ball go. It was a ridiculous pitch that landed almost four feet away from the plate on the left side. Everyone laughed, including Christy.

"If that's your best," Jaeson heckled, "we don't want to see your worst."

"I was just testing you," Christy called back. "Wanted to see if you would swing at anything. Here comes a good one."

Christy pitched a nice, slow ball straight over home plate. With Jaeson's help, the girl smacked the ball almost all the way to the woods. Everyone cheered as she ran the bases with Jaeson by her side. The other three runners came home with hoots and hollers.

A fielder threw the ball to second base just as Jaeson and the girl touched third. Now it was a battle to see if they could make it home. Jaeson picked up the girl, carrying her under his arm like a football, as he charged home. They made it a few seconds before the ball did, and Jaeson put the girl down firmly on home plate, like an explorer planting a flag and claiming the land.

A small crowd of campers had gathered, and everyone was still cheering when the next girl stepped up to bat. "I want Jaeson to help me too," she said.

"Naw, you can do it yourself. Go ahead and try," Jaeson coached from the sidelines.

With the first pitch, the girl looked as though she deliberately swung and missed. Perhaps she hoped her lack of coordination would bring Jaeson to her side.

"Come on," he called out. "I know you can do better than that."

She positioned the bat over her shoulder and turned to Christy with a fierce look on her face. Christy wanted to laugh. This girl was taking the game more seriously than it was intended. Christy gave her an easy, low ball, and the girl hit a grounder that dribbled right back to Christy. Watching the girl run to first base out of the corner of her eye, Christy made sure she was almost there before snatching up the grounder and tossing it to first base. The girl was safe. By the look on her face, she was quite proud of herself.

In the distance, they heard the camp bell ringing, which was their signal to go to the evening meeting. Everyone groaned. Christy's girls complained they didn't have a chance to bat.

"Can we finished our game tomorrow?" they asked.

"Sure," Christy agreed. "How about tomorrow right after lunch?"

"You were too nice to them," Sara said. "You were trying to make them win."

"She would pitch the same way if you were up to bat," Jaeson said, coming to Christy's defense and joining them as they headed back to main camp. "That's what counselors are supposed to do, be fair to everybody."

The girl Jaeson had helped around the bases now had a hold of his arm and looked as though she intended to remain attached permanently to him. Sara grabbed Jaeson's other arm.

Looking up at him with her ginger eyes, she pleaded, "Will you play with us tomorrow afternoon? Pleeeease?"

"Sure," Jaeson said, catching Christy's eye and giving her a big smile. "Christy and I make a good team, don't you think?"

That comment prompted a round of agreement from the girls, including Jocelyn's bright statement, "Why don't you two get married? Then you could do this every day for the rest of your lives."

"Hey, yeah!" Jeanine agreed. "You could build a little cabin over there in the woods, and we'd all come and stay with you. You could take us canoeing and play baseball everyday."

Christy was too embarrassed to look at Jaeson, but she could feel his amused glance. Fortunately they were back at camp and could file into the meeting hall with the rest of the campers. The singing started a few minutes after they walked in. Christy's girls, full of energy, sang loudly, nudging each other and making up their own hand motions to go along with the motions they had already learned. Christy looked across the room and noticed Jaeson sitting with his boys. He turned and gazed back at her, giving one of his thumbs-up signs. She smiled back, hoping her girls hadn't noticed.

Then Christy spotted a film projector set up in the back. She remembered Dean Ferrill telling them at the counselors meeting they had a movie for the kids tonight that should get them thinking. At devos that night the counselors were supposed to take advantage of the film's message to see if any of their campers wanted to make a commitment to Christ.

The lights were out, and the movie started. Christy felt a firm hand on her shoulder. Jaeson whispered in her ear, "Come with me."

Christy slipped out without her girls noticing and followed Jaeson. As soon as the door to the meeting hall closed behind them, he took Christy's hand and said, "Time for your canoe lesson."

"Now?"

Jaeson, still holding her hand, pulled her along with him as he jogged toward the lake. "Now's the best time. Right after sunset. The water is smooth, and it's nice and quiet."

"But are you sure this is okay?" Christy puffed. She couldn't help but feel they were sneaking off, leaving their campers behind. They would get in trouble for this, she just knew it.

"We'll be back before the movie is over. It won't be a problem. Trust me."

Jaeson kept a firm hold on her hand as they wound through the woods. They arrived at the boat shack winded. He had the wild look of an adventurer in his eyes when he handed Christy her life jacket and paddle. She still felt they were doing something wrong and would get caught.

"Are you sure this is okay, Jaeson?"

"You want to learn to canoe, don't you? Now's your golden opportunity. Just look at the lake. Isn't it beautiful?"

She had to admit Jaeson was right. The lake looked like the polished floor of a ballet studio, with the fading golden lights of the summer evening dancing across it.

"Get in," Jaeson ordered when he had positioned the canoe halfway into the water.

Christy carefully balanced her way to the front bench and held on, trying to keep the canoe steady. Jaeson dropped his full weight on the back bench and used his paddle to push off from shore.

Suddenly it was quiet. The only sounds were the calm water rippling up against the canoe's side and the evening chorus of bullfrogs and crickets along the shore.

"Jaeson," Christy whispered, "are you sure we should be out here?"

"Relax, will you? I've done this a bunch of times." Then Jaeson's voice became softer and he said, "Isn't it beautiful out here? I love this. Come on, relax, Christy. I promise tonight will be the highlight of your whole week."

Christy's fingers clutched the paddle in her lap. Her eyes darted back and forth across the darkening waters as they headed for the middle of the lake.

Relax, huh?

CHAPTER EIGHT

Moonlight Picnic

When they reached the middle of the lake, Jaeson said, "Now, the first thing you need to know is how to hold the paddle. I noticed you were holding it like this today."

He showed Christy in the dim light that he had both hands on the neck of the paddle. "You need to put one hand on the top like this and the other right about here."

Christy held up her paddle and followed his instructions.

"Good. I knew you would be a fast learner. When you're in the canoe alone, you have to paddle from the back if you want to control which way it goes. You were trying to steer it from the front this afternoon. Watch."

Jaeson dipped his paddle in the water on the right side, and as he gave a mighty stroke, the canoe lunged forward. Another stroke on the left side, and the canoe charged again. Jaeson kept the canoe going straight from his control point at the back.

"You try it," Jaeson said. "Turn around and face me, and your end will become the back of the canoe."

Christy lifted one long leg and tried to swing it over to the other side without tipping the canoe. It felt terribly awkward. She managed to get both legs over and sat facing Jaeson. It was too dark to see his expression clearly, but she thought he was smiling at her.

Does he think I'm a klutz or what? I can't tell if he's smiling at me or laughing at me.

"Are you right-handed?" Jaeson asked.

"Yes, why?"

"I have a theory that you'll have more strength paddling on your left side, because your right hand will be on top of the paddle and that's your strongest. So start your paddle on the left side. Remember to put your hand on top."

Christy followed his instructions.

"Good. Always start with a strong stroke and then switch to the other side and give it another strong stroke."

Christy did, and Jaeson praised her. "See how different it feels when you're at the back of the canoe? You have much more control."

"You're right," Christy said. "Thanks for the lesson."

Jaeson started to scan the treetops on the other side of the lake. "It won't be here for another ten minutes," he said. "Good thing I brought provisions for us."

"What won't be here?"

"You'll see. Thirsty?" Jaeson reached for a bundle on the floor in the center of the canoe.

Christy had noticed it when she had climbed in but thought it was just a blanket. He undid the bundle and revealed a variety of "provisions."

"What's that?" Christy asked.

"Our moonlight picnic," he said, placing a lantern onto the center seat. He lit the wick inside. Jaeson pulled out a glass and scooped up some lake water and placed it next to the lantern. He picked up a dozen squashed wildflowers from the bundle and dunked them in the vase.

Christy laughed at his creativity. "This is charming, Jaeson."

"Charming?" he repeated. "It's been called many things, but I think I like charming the best so far."

Christy took it from his comment that during his years as a camp counselor, he had taken more than one girl out for a moonlight picnic. She wondered if tonight was any different for him. Was she special to him? Or was she just another girl counselor he could flirt with for the week? She wanted to be his favorite, the only girl he had ever done this with. She wanted it to be romantic and as wonderful for him as it was for her.

Jaeson handed Christy an opened bottle of mineral water and a napkin.

"Thank you, kind sir," she said, playing along with the fun.

"And now for the best part," Jaeson announced. "Peanut butter cookies saved from Sunday night!"

He handed Christy a cookie that was about seventy-five percent there.

"That's the biggest one," he said. "They get a little crumbly after the second day."

Christy laughed. "This is great, Jaeson! How fun. Thanks for bringing me out here."

She bit into the cookie and listened to the sound of the lake gently lapping at the side of the canoe.

"Oh, I almost forgot." Jaeson rummaged through the bundle and came up with a Walkman. He popped in a tape, cranked the volume all the way up, and balanced it on the middle seat with the earphones pointed in Christy's direction. The music came out soft and just loud enough.

"A little music," he said.

Christy felt like giggling; this was all so fun. A breeze blew over them, bringing with it the cool, pungent smell of the moss with just a hint of coconut tanning lotion.

"So," Jaeson said, leaning back slightly and taking a bite out of his cookie, "tell me your dreams."

"What?"

"What do you wish? What are your dreams for the future?"

Christy was caught off-guard. Whenever she dreamed of the future, the dreams included Todd. She couldn't tell that to Jaeson. Not here with the music and lantern light and everything.

"I don't know if I really have any dreams or wishes for the future," she answered.

"Sure you do. You have to. Everyone has to have a dream. Do you want to hear mine?"

"Sure," Christy said.

"I want to be a pilot. I want to fly my own plane. Not those big commercial airplanes or military jets. I want a little plane. I'd even be happy as a crop duster. That's my wish."

"Have you taken any flying lessons?" Christy asked.

"No, but I have some information on them. I'm saving up my money, because they're not cheap. Maybe by this fall I'll start lessons."

"That's a good dream," Christy said, taking a sip from her bottle. "I bet you'll make a great pilot."

"Your turn," Jaeson said. "What's your dream?"

"Well, I only thought of one thing. I've never told anyone this before, I don't think."

"You can tell me. All secrets shared on moonlight picnics are safe with me." Jaeson reached for another cookie and listened intently, waiting for her answer.

"I'd like to go to England. To Europe, actually. I've always wanted to visit a real castle and go for a ride in a gondola in Venice. That's my dream," Christy said, feeling brave.

"That's a jolly good dream," Jaeson said with a British accent. "You do have a bit of a Mary Poppins look about you. I'm sure your wish will come true."

Just then he spotted something over the top of Christy's head. It was easier to see his expression now, and Christy noticed his face lighting up with delight.

"Here he comes," Jaeson said. "Look!"

Christy turned around and saw what Jaeson was so excited about. The moon, a big, fat, buttery ball, had just popped over the treetops and was dripping its golden light onto the lake.

"Right on time," Jaeson said, gently paddling the canoe around so Christy wouldn't have to look over her shoulder.

"It's so beautiful!" Christy whispered as they watched the moon rise over the lake and shine on them like a searchlight. Everything around them took on a hazy, amber glow, and for some reason it felt warmer.

They sat in silence, enjoying the night show and listening to the muted melodies floating from the Walkman. Christy knew Jaeson had been right when he said this would be the highlight of her week. Still, as wonderful and romantic and peaceful as everything was, thoughts of Todd crept into the fantasy evening.

There's nothing wrong with me being here with Jaeson and enjoying this romantic moment with him. It doesn't change anything between Todd and me.

Just then Jaeson leaned toward Christy, his hand reaching for her face.

Is he going to kiss me? What should I do?

Jaeson's hand brushed against her cheek. "There. You had some cookie crumbs on your cheek."

"Oh," Christy's hand flew to her cheek and brushed away a few tiny crumbs Jaeson's hand had missed. Her skin felt hot to her touch, and she hoped Jaeson couldn't see her blushing in the moonlight.

"When do we need to leave to get back before we're missed?" she asked, trying not to sound as nervous as she felt.

"Oh, about now. Are you sure you want to go? This is the most peace and quiet you'll have for the rest of the week."

Christy wanted to stay. She wanted to float on the quiet lake for hours and stare at the moon and share her secret dreams with Jaeson. She wanted the fantasy to go on and on. But inwardly the struggle was growing. Should she be here, alone with Jaeson? Would they get in trouble for leaving the meeting? Would she do or say anything with Jaeson that she would later regret?

"I guess we should go back," Christy said with a sigh. "This has been wonderful, Jaeson. The music, the flowers, the moonlight. I love it. I loved being here with you."

"Thanks. I'm glad you liked it." He extinguished the lantern light. "I'll take you back. Remember, though, it was your choice, not mine."

He lifted the bunch of flowers from the vase and handed them to Christy. "To remember me by."

She took them and said, "I'll keep them, Jaeson, and I know I'll never forget you or tonight."

She could see his smile in the moonlight and felt content and a little relieved things had gone just as far as they had and no farther.

Dipping her paddle into the water, she asked, "You want me to practice paddling us back to shore?"

"Good idea. Remember to start on your left side."

Christy tried to remember all Jaeson's pointers as she plunged the paddle deep into the water and headed them for shore. It was a lot easier than her afternoon experience had been, and in no time, Jaeson's end of the canoe scraped up onto the gravel.

"Excellent," Jaeson said, hopping out and pulling them up on shore. "I'll put the gear away if you want to head on back. Or you can wait for me if you want."

The thought of wandering through the dark woods by herself didn't thrill Christy, so she helped Jaeson put the stuff back where it belonged. He stuffed the picnic bundle into a corner in the boat shack. Christy couldn't help but wonder if it would sit there until next week when Jaeson would take another girl counselor out on the lake.

He took her by the hand again, and they hurried back to the meeting hall where the campers were just beginning to stream out the open doors and run for their snacks.

"See?" Jaeson said, letting go of her hand and joining the throng headed for the mess hall. "No problem."

Christy almost believed everything was okay until devotions in her cabin that night when she was supposed to discuss the movie with her girls. As they all started to jabber about it, Christy had no idea what they were talking about. Quickly taking another direction, she asked the girls to be quiet and listen so she could tell them her testimony.

"Why do they call it a testimony, Teach?" Amy asked.

"Well, I guess because you're telling something that happened to you and you're letting people know that what you're saying is true," Christy explained. Then she went on to tell the girls how she had grown up in a Christian home.

"How can a house be a Christian?" Sara popped off.

The other girls laughed, and Christy calmed them down, saying, "Of course a house can't be a Christian. What I meant is both of my parents are Christians, so I grew up going to church."

"Me too," Ruthie said, and several other girls chimed in that their parents were Christians too.

"It wasn't enough for me to just know about God," Christy said. "I had to invite Him into my life. I did that when I was fifteen. I prayed and asked God to forgive all my sins and to come into my life. He did, and since that time I've slowly been changing and becoming more the person God wants me to be."

"How can there be a Christian school?" Sara asked. "The people who go there could be Christians, but the school can't become a Christian."

The other girls joined in with their opinions on the difference between a school of Christians and a Christian school. Christy felt certain none of them had heard her testimony, and even if some of them had, it didn't seem to matter much to them.

"Okay, girls. That's enough. I'm going to turn out the lights, and everyone needs to be in her sleeping bag." She snapped off the light and climbed into bed.

"Now I'm going to pray, and if any of you wants to pray, you can. We'll all be silent for a little bit so anyone who wants to can pray, and then after a while I'll close, okay? Let's pray."

It was silent for about two seconds, and then one of the girls gave a loud snort, which prompted lots of muffled giggles. Then someone else did her best to manufacture a belch. Jocelyn whispered, "Stop kicking my bed, Sara."

"Girls," Christy said firmly, "we are praying."

It became silent. Completely silent. None of the girls prayed, so Christy jumped in after two minutes of silence. She prayed specifically for each of the girls, the way they did in the counselors meetings. Then she prayed for the other campers, the counselors, the camp staff, and the campers who would be coming next week.

Her prayer lasted more than five minutes, and when she finished, not one girl was still awake.

Well, she thought, *that's one way to get them to sleep at night!*

Christy fell asleep immediately and had wonderful dreams about being in a row boat on a placid lake with swans swimming around her. Behind her was a huge, storybook castle. She held a lacy parasol and twirled it with her white-gloved fingers. Across from her sat a man dressed in a tuxedo who was pouring tea into a china cup. When he asked if she would like one lump of sugar or two, he looked up, and she saw that it was Todd.

When she woke up with the alarm at 6:00 the next morning, she felt rested. Bouncing out of bed, she headed to the rest room for a brisk morning shower. Jessica was already there, and Christy told her about her new devotional tactic for praying the girls to sleep.

"The only bad part was they didn't pay attention when I gave my testimony, and none of them prayed. I don't think any of my girls are interested in spiritual things."

Jessica wrapped a towel around her wet hair, and pouring some astringent on a cotton ball, she began her facial-cleansing routine. "I think the next step is for you to spend time with each of them one-on-one and find out where they are."

"How can I do that? It's Thursday already. That's not much time. Besides, what do I say? 'Let's have some quality time. We've got three minutes. So tell me if you're saved or not, and if you want to be or not.' "

Jessica laughed. "Not like that, Christy. Just sit down with each of them individually, tell them you care about them, and ask if there's anything they want to talk about. We don't know which ones are ready to give their hearts to the Lord and which ones aren't. God knows. All we need to do is give them an opportunity to talk about it and offer to answer their questions."

Christy combed through her wet hair. "You're right. I'll figure out a way to get together with each of them. I hope you know that if you weren't here giving me all this good advice, I'd be completely lost."

"I'm sure you would do fine," Jessica said. "I'm glad we're here together, though. I want to be sure to get your address so we can stay in contact after camp."

"Me too," Christy agreed. "My friend Katie is never going to believe I said this, but I'm glad I came. It's been a great week."

"It's not over yet! We still have to live through the counselor hunt tomorrow."

The hunt was the first thing they discussed at the meeting that morning.

"I suggest," Dean Ferrill said, "that you each take a hike over to the other side of the lake sometime today and scope out a hiding place. This will help save a lot of time tomorrow when you get over there."

Since Christy had promised the girls she would pitch at their softball game after lunch, she wasn't sure when she would have a chance to hunt for a spot. Fortunately it was hotter than usual that afternoon, and after three innings, both teams were ready to quit and find a cooler sport. The minute one of them suggested volleyball in the pool, they all disappeared, leaving Jaeson and Christy alone to put away the equipment.

"You coming over to the pool?" Jaeson asked.

"Actually, I thought I'd better find myself a good hiding place across the lake."

"Good idea. I'll go with you. I can show you some places I've used before."

They walked around the lake rather than taking a canoe. At

one spot where the trail became narrow, Jaeson reached his hand behind him, offering it to Christy. She felt comfortable holding Jaeson's hand.

"Here's one spot I used last year," Jaeson said, stopping and pointing straight up.

"Where?" Christy asked.

"Up there. This is an easy tree to climb. It was a lot of fun, because the kids never thought to look up even though I showered them with pine needles."

"I'm not much of a tree climber," Christy said hesitantly. "Do you have any other suggestions?"

"Sure. Follow me."

Jaeson led her through the woods, pointing out five possible hiding spots. She liked the last one best and decided that was the one for her. It was a hollowed-out tree trunk behind a huge tree that grew close to the trail. The campers would have to go off the trail and around the tree to find her. She thought it would be good to bring a towel along so she wouldn't have to sit on the moldy bark inside the tree.

Jaeson took her hand again and began to lead her back. He stopped at the good climbing tree and said, "I think I'll try going up again this year. Worked great last year."

He then coached Christy on canoe strategy. She loved this feeling. The birds were singing above them, the shimmering lake was peeking at them from behind the trees, and she was on an afternoon walk hand-in-hand with the cutest counselor at camp. This is what Christy dreamed camp would be like. Nothing of her previous life seemed to matter now. She had two more days at Camp Wildwood, and she intended to enjoy every minute of them.

CHAPTER NINE

View From a Hollow Tree

At dinner that night Jocelyn wasn't eating. Christy asked her if she felt okay.

"My stomach hurts," she said.

Christy felt her forehead and said, "You feel pretty warm. Let's get you over to the nurse's office."

Turning to Jaeson, who sat behind her as usual, Christy asked, "Can you keep an eye on my girls? This one needs to see the nurse."

With her arm around Jocelyn, Christy escorted her from the noisy mess hall and across the grounds to the nurse's small white building.

When they were only a few yards away, Jocelyn said, "I think I have to throw up."

"Can you make it to those bushes?" Christy asked, helping Jocelyn walk a little faster.

They made it just in time for Jocelyn to be sick. Christy turned away and held her breath. This was a part of camp counseling she hadn't planned on. Rummaging through her pockets, she found a tissue. Still holding her breath, she held it out to Jocelyn and said, "Here."

Jocelyn groaned and started to cry as she wiped off her mouth. "I feel awful!"

"We're almost there, honey," Christy said, wrapping her arm back around Jocelyn and coaxing the sobbing girl along.

Fortunately the nurse must have heard them coming because she opened the door and helped Jocelyn to a clean cot.

"Her stomach hurts," Christy explained. "She threw up out there in the bushes."

"You poor little thing," the nurse said, placing her hand on Jocelyn's forehead. "What did you eat today?"

"She didn't eat any dinner," Christy said.

"What about during free time? Did you have any snacks?"

Jocelyn slowly nodded her head and listed half a dozen snack foods and types of candy bars she'd eaten.

The nurse placed a cool washcloth on Jocelyn's forehead and whispered to Christy, "Sounds like a case of junk food overload. I'll give her something to settle her stomach, and she'll be fine."

Christy patted Jocelyn on the arm and said, "You do what the nurse says, and I'll check on you later, okay?"

She was about to slip out when the nurse said, "Could you do me a favor? Would you fill up the bucket on the side of the building and then wash down the site where she vomited?"

Christy shuddered as she doused the spot with a bucket of water. This was definitely the part of being a counselor that she could do without. For good measure, she filled a second bucket and poured it over the area so no signs of the accident remained.

I'm glad I got her out of the mess hall when I did!

The doors to the mess hall opened, and the Camp Wildwood wild campers scattered to make use of their short free time before the evening meeting.

Oh, great, dinner's over, and I didn't finish eating. Actually, I don't feel like eating anymore.

Christy had planned to spend time with her girls individually today, but with the baseball game and the walk with Jaeson, the afternoon had flown. Jeanine was the first of her girls she spotted exiting the dining hall. She caught up with her and asked, "Do you want to do something?"

Jeanine looked at her funny. "Like what?"

"I don't know. Go for a walk, sit by the lake, and talk."

"Why?"

"Well, just so we can have some time together," Christy said, scrambling for a better approach.

"We've been together all week," Jeanine said. "We're bunk-mates even."

"I know, I just thought maybe, well . . . never mind."

"No," Jeanine said, clutching Christy's arm. "We can do something if you want."

Now Christy wasn't sure who was the leader and who was the follower. "Why don't we just go out in the woods and talk. I know where there's a bench not far from here."

"Okay," Jeanine said cheerfully. "If that'll make you feel better."

Christy led Jeanine to the bench. She had planned her opening line during their walk and sprang it on Jeanine. "I want you to know that I think you're wonderful, I care about you, and I want to know if you have any questions about God."

Jeanine looked at her a moment before answering. "Nope."

"Okay, that's fine." Christy had no idea where to go next with her big witnessing opportunity. "So you feel as though everything between you and God is fine?"

"Yep. My parents prayed with me when I was little, Jesus lives in my heart, and I know I'm going to heaven. Do you think you could braid my hair like that other counselor Jessica braids her girls' hair?"

"I could try," Christy floundered.

Why don't any of these girls want to talk about spiritual things?

"Good," Jeanine said, turning her back to Christy and scrounging in her pocket. "I have a rubber band here." She proceeded to extract at least two dozen rubber bands from her pocket.

"What are all these for?" Christy asked, trying to smooth Jeanine's matted mane with her fingernails before she pulled all the pieces together in a French braid.

"Jessica told me to try giving something to Nick instead of taking stuff from him, you know? I tried it with the leather bracelet, but you know how that turned out. So now I'm giving him something else. A rubber band in the back of the head whenever he's not looking. He still doesn't know it's me."

Christy was glad Jeanine couldn't see her face. She couldn't repress her smile.

"How come guys don't start to like girls at the same age as girls start to like boys?" Jeanine asked, patiently holding her head still.

"I don't know. Maybe God is giving the girls an extra year or two to polish up on their manners. That way, when the guys are old enough to be interested in them, they'll be the kind of girls worth being interested in."

"I never thought of it that way," Jeanine said, genuinely persuaded. "Will you teach me how to have better manners?"

"Sure, if you'd like. Hand me a rubber band." Christy tied off the end of Jeanine's braid.

Then Jeanine turned eagerly to face Christy. With her hair off her face, Jeanine was a pretty little girl.

"First, I'd say lose the rubber bands. I don't think that's going to help with Nick at all. Next, try to eat with your mouth closed and not to talk when you have food in your mouth."

"What else?" Jeanine asked.

"Well, sitting up straight always helps."

Jeanine immediately straightened her back and held her head up high. "Like this?"

"Yes, that's very good. I might mention screaming next. There's a place for screaming. Like in the pool or on a roller coaster. But for the most part you don't need to scream a lot during the day just for the sake of screaming."

Jeanine nodded solemnly. "What else?"

"That's a good start. Always try to say kind things and be considerate of others."

Jeanine beamed, looking anxious to take off and try some of her new charm techniques on Nick. Just as she was about to hop up, Christy touched her arm and asked, "May I bless you, Jeanine?"

"Bless me? But I didn't sneeze."

Months ago, one chilly morning on the beach, Todd had placed his hand on Christy's forehead and blessed her. At the time she didn't want the blessing and didn't receive it well. But his act had stayed with her all this time. For some reason Christy felt the urge to bless this girl, who was blossoming into a young lady right before her eyes.

"Just close your eyes," Christy instructed. She then placed her hand across Jeanine's forehead and said, "Jeanine, the Lord bless you and keep you. The Lord make His face to shine upon you and give you His peace. And may you always love Jesus first, above all else."

Jeanine opened her sparkling eyes. A big smile spread across her face. "That was neat!" she said. "What does the 'love Jesus above all else' mean?"

"It means in every situation you face as you're growing up, may you fall in love with Jesus and love Him more than you love anything else."

"Thanks, Christy," Jeanine said, hopping up and impulsively giving Christy a hug. "You're the best counselor in the whole world!" Then off she ran down the trail.

Christy sat for a moment, thinking about the advice she had just given. She wished she could say she already had that kind of love for Jesus. She did love Him, but she wanted to love Him even more. Todd once said that was good because it meant she was "hungering and thirsting after righteousness."

Even though her talk with Jeanine hadn't gone the way she had planned, she felt good. She had given Jeanine what she needed, and maybe the blessing would help Jeanine feel loved.

Christy sat with Amy, Sara, and Ruthie at the evening meeting. She was glad Amy and Sara had included Ruthie into their little group. Christy quietly told Amy and Sara in the cabin that night that she liked the way they were being good friends with each other and with other girls in their cabin. Both girls looked pleased and proud.

For devotions, Christy read them her favorite psalm, Psalm 139. Then she talked for a few minutes about how much God loved each of them and how much He wanted them to promise their hearts to Him.

Christy felt as though her "message" had gone well and anticipated lots of discussion afterwards—and hopefully a conversion or two. She gave her closing line and waited for their responses.

All of them had fallen asleep except Sara.

Christy tried to hide her disappointment as she asked Sara, "Do you have any questions?"

"Yes," Sara said, "has Jaeson kissed you yet?"

"No, of course not."

"Why not? You like him and he likes you."

"Sara, that's not enough of a reason to kiss a guy. When you give away kisses, you're giving a little part of your heart that you can never take back. You have to be careful that you don't give away too many pieces too soon or to the wrong person."

"You *have* been kissed before, haven't you? What was it like? Did you close your eyes?"

"Sara, let's talk about this later. I think we both need some sleep, okay?"

Christy pulled up her sleeping bag over her ears and only heard a muffled response from Sara about how nobody ever wanted to talk about it. Promising herself she would talk to Sara tomorrow about kissing, Christy fell asleep.

She floated in and out of a confusing dream in which Jaeson tried to kiss her and she didn't know how to respond.

Friday dawned overcast and chilly. It was the first morning Christy put on jeans instead of shorts. She passed on the chance to have an invigorating shower and pulled her hair back in a ponytail rather than washing it. Her neck was stiff. She felt as if she had been at camp for six months instead of six days.

Everyone at breakfast seemed on edge too. Perhaps it was because this was the last full day of camp or because it was cold and rainy outside. Whatever it was, the mood hung over the camp all morning. At lunch two of her girls argued over the last half of a grilled cheese sandwich until one of them fell backwards with her chair. If Christy hadn't rushed over in time to hold them back, there would have been a major fight.

"Here," Jessica said, offering Christy's table a plate of sandwiches. "My girls aren't very hungry."

Jocelyn grabbed the first sandwich. Ever since her recovery early that morning, she had been eating everything in sight.

Jessica then confided in Christy over the roar of the savage campers, "I don't like it when they get this way before the counselor hunt. You would think they were out for blood!"

"Our blood, I suppose," Christy answered.

Jessica nodded and headed back to her table of sassy whiners, who kept asking when they could leave so they could go to the snack shack and buy candy bars.

The instant they burst out of the dining room, the sun popped through the clouds and looked as though it would stay around all afternoon. Within minutes Christy felt boiling hot in her jeans and sweatshirt and decided to change into shorts before the counselor hunt. She also wanted to take along a towel to sit on inside her tree.

The cabin was a disastrous mess. The girls hadn't worked on it at all during cabin cleanup, and since Christy was in the counselors meeting during that time, she hadn't been there to motivate them. They had lost points for the mess, but her girls didn't seem to care.

Christy hurried down to the lake. Six canoes were lined up on the shore with a bright flag mounted on the stern of each. Christy was assigned the canoe with the orange flag and tied the matching orange strip of cloth to her waist. She was to relinquish this sash to the first camper who found her.

Dean Ferrill gave the rest of the instructions, and Christy mounted her "trusty steed" with a surge of excitement. With paddle in hand, she waited along with the other counselors for the signal.

"On your mark, get set . . . ," Dean Ferrill's shrill whistle blew, and Christy plunged her paddle into the water on the left side, just as Jaeson had told her. She got a good, swift start and was ahead of the other girls by several yards in no time. With each stroke she felt the muscles in her upper arms stretching and letting her know she was giving it all she had.

Christy was glad she had changed into her cut-off jeans and her Camp Wildwood T-shirt when she felt the sun beating down on the tops of her legs. The sun's intensity seemed double because of the reflection off the water.

From the shore behind her, Christy could hear the shouts from the campers. They were to stay put until the first counselor's canoe touched the shore on the opposite side. Then they were released to run around the lake and find the counselors.

Jessica was right. From the way the campers' yells and screams echoed across the lake, they did sound as though they were out for blood.

Near the middle of the lake, the three guys overtook Christy and passed her, the three of them stroking in unison, with their canoes lined up neck and neck.

Then Jessica passed her and called out, "Keep going, Christy. We're almost there."

Christy paddled harder, keeping her canoe straight and aiming for a nice, big open spot on the shore. Jaeson hit the shore first. Then Mike, Jessica, and Bob. Right behind them, Christy's canoe made the welcome sound of hitting mud and gravel. She hopped out, pulled her canoe to shore, and ran with soggy tennis shoes to her hiding spot in the hollowed-out tree.

She found the tree with no problem but realized she had left her towel in the canoe. From the echoing sounds of the wild campers running around the lake, she knew she didn't have enough time to go back to retrieve it.

With her muddy tennis shoe, she tried to scrape out some of the gunk on the floor of her hiding place. It seemed she was leaving more mud inside than she was managing to get moldy bark out. The campers' voices sounded closer.

Christy gave up and wedged herself into the triangular hideout. Drawing her long legs up close to her chest, she wrapped her arms around them and tried to make herself as small as possible. Then she tried to slow her breathing down to a calmer pace.

The inside of the tree was actually kind of interesting. A few inches from her face, the wood appeared to be rippled in several layers around the opening of the trunk. It smelled musty but in an earthy way that didn't bother her.

As a child, Christy had always liked stories about woodland critters who lived in the trees. She pictured one of her storybook elves or dwarfs being delighted to use her hideout as his home.

The first camper's footsteps came pounding down the trail right behind Christy's tree. She held her breath but feared her loudly pounding heart would give her away. Several more ran by, yelling and screaming, and Christy actually felt frightened. Not that they would find her; that was the game. But what if they were so wild this afternoon that they thought it a good idea to tie her up and leave her there?

She wiggled slightly, trying to improve her position. The bark was poking her and she felt tingles up and down her legs, probably from them falling asleep. As her eyes adjusted to the darkness of her cave, Christy realized that the bark in front of her face appeared to be moving. She looked closely and discovered a nonstop string of red ants marching across the entrance, only inches from her face.

With great control she kept herself from screaming or even moving an inch. Another hoard of campers thundered behind her down the trail. She kept silent. Then she felt that tingly sensation from her legs move up her arms and onto her hands. At that moment, she realized she was covered with ants.

"Yiiiiii!" she screeched, ejecting herself from the tree and jumping around in the woods, slapping her arms and legs in a futile effort to get the ants off her.

Two girls from Jessica's cabin found her in the midst of her furious dance and ventured carefully toward her. "Can we have your orange strip?" they asked cautiously.

"Come and get it," Christy said, still shaking and stamping her feet. Dozens of red ants fell to the ground. But it wasn't enough.

One of the girls timidly drew near and snatched the end of the orange cloth. As she pulled it from Christy's waist, another dozen ants emerged and raced down the cloth and up the girl's hand.

Now she too was screaming and shaking, doing the Christy ant-dance.

"What are you two doing?" the other girl asked. "I'm taking this back to the other side!" She grabbed the orange cloth, shook it out, and took off running.

"You're supposed to get in your canoe and beat her back," the girl explained.

"I can't," Christy wailed. "I still have ants in my pants!"

"Maybe if you run to the canoe, they'll fall out, and then if there are any left, you can sit on them and squish them all."

Christy was close to tears. "They sting. My legs feel like they're on fire!"

"Then jump in the water," the girl suggested. "Look, they bit me, too." She held out her hand, revealing a baker's dozen red spots.

"This is awful!" Christy cried. "Are you okay?"

"I'm going to go to the nurse."

"Good idea," Christy said, slapping herself on the legs as she raced to the canoe. Then, because the cool lake water seemed like the only thing that could possibly stop the stinging, she jumped in and came up soaking.

"Christy!" Jaeson called out as he ran up and pushed off the canoe next to hers. "What are you doing? Get in your canoe! Come on! I'll push you off. We can paddle together."

In spite of her misery, she jumped into her canoe and let Jaeson push her off, knowing she had no time to explain. With quivering arms, she numbly followed Jaeson's shouted-out instructions.

"Paddle left. Paddle right. Come on, Christy, faster!"

Her hair was dripping in her face, and her legs were shivering and burning at the same time. She glanced at her arms and saw the red marks beginning to swell.

"Paddle left. Paddle right. Faster!"

"I can't keep up!" she cried out to Jaeson. "You go ahead."

Jaeson pulled out in front of her, and with a quick thumbs-up, his strong arms shot his canoe through the water like a well-aimed arrow. He made it to shore and planted his flag before his runner arrived. Since he was the first counselor back and most of the campers were still on the other side, it seemed a hollow victory with so few to cheer for him.

Christy paddled slowly but steadily, trying with all her might to ignore the increasingly painful stinging in her arms and legs. She still was a ways from shore when her arms gave out. "Come on, Christy," Jaeson called. "You can do it! Paddle left. Paddle right."

She tried, but it seemed pointless. Her chest was heaving from being so winded, and her head began to throb. The breeze nudged her a few feet closer to shore as she tried to catch her breath.

"Come on, Christy," Jaeson called again. "Your runner is almost here! Only a few more paddles."

Christy stroked three times on each side of the canoe and seemed to drift backwards rather than forward. She looked to the shore and saw Jaeson waving his arms and coaching her to give it full steam.

Just then the girl with Christy's orange strip in her hand shot through the woods and crumpled on the gravel as she plunged her strip of fabric into the hole meant for Christy's flag. The score was now counselors One, campers One.

Hanging her head, Christy realized how dizzy she felt. Hearing a splash in the water, she looked up and saw Jaeson swimming out to her canoe. He took hold of the rope in the front and towed her the twenty more feet to shore.

"I'm sorry," Christy apologized, reaching for Jaeson's hand to help her out.

"Christy, what happened? You're covered with red spots!"

"Ants," she breathed out, feeling completely exhausted. Her soggy tennis shoes slipped on the gravel, and Jaeson caught her just before she fell.

"You're going to the nurse," he said. "Put your arm around my shoulder. I'll help you walk to camp."

"Are you okay?" Dean Ferrill asked when he came over and saw Christy's polka-dotted skin.

"I'll take her to the nurse," Jaeson offered. "Cheer the rest of the counselors in for us, okay?"

Limping and leaning against Jaeson for support, Christy felt ridiculous to have been defeated by a bunch of stupid ants. She said nothing all the way to the infirmary. Jaeson talked the whole time about other mishaps he had seen at camp over the years, everything from broken collarbones to split lips. Somehow nothing he said made her feel better.

"Red ants," Jaeson told the nurse when she opened her door. The nurse took a quick look at Christy's arms and said, "Oh, my, this doesn't look good."

"Wait till you see this," Christy said, exposing the back of her raw legs to the nurse.

"Oh, my gracious! What did you do, girl, sit on their convention center?"

"I think so," Christy said, trying hard to smile but not having much success.

"I'll check on you later," Jaeson promised and left Christy in the hands of the sympathetic nurse.

"Let's get you in the tub and make sure all those critters are off you," the nurse said. "I hope you didn't have any special plans for the evening, because I'm afraid you're not going anywhere for a while."

A few minutes later Christy lowered herself into the lukewarm tub, anticipating a soothing sensation. Instead, the water felt like a thousand needles were plunged into her flesh. She itched like crazy.

"Whatever you do," the nurse called to her through the closed door, "don't scratch. I've put something in the water to draw out the poison. If you scratch, you'll only spread it."

The camper from the woods with the ant bites on her hand had arrived, and the nurse was checking her hand as Christy soaked.

"I hope you know," Christy called back, "that this is about the worst torture a person could ever go through."

"I know. I'm sorry. But it *will* help. Trust me."

At that uncomfortable moment, Christy knew she had no other choice.

CHAPTER TEN

Sara's Promise

After drying off and putting on some clean clothes, Christy lay on her stomach on the infirmary cot so the nurse could smear her spotted legs with a cold, gooey lotion. She wanted to cry. This had to be one of her life's all-time worst experiences.

Covering Christy with a sheet, the nurse instructed, "Don't move. Stay on your stomach and try to get some rest."

It's funny, but I never thought much about wanting to sleep on my side or my back until she told me I could only lie on my stomach.

Christy wiggled and clenched her teeth. How could she rest? The lotion stung almost as bad as the ant bites.

"How's the patient?" Dean Ferrill's voice called from the front door.

"Trying to rest. She was attacked pretty severely," the nurse said. "You can go on in and see her if you like."

The dean had to walk all the way around to the front of Christy's cot and squat down on one knee so he could look her in the face.

"You okay?" he asked with such a tender tone that Christy couldn't hold back the tears.

"I'm fine," her voice said, but her tears told him differently.

She blinked, trying to stop from crying. Then she realized she couldn't use her hands to wipe the tears from her face because the pink lotion would get in her eyes.

"Here," Dean Ferrill said, recognizing her dilemma and reaching for a tissue. He wiped her eyes for her. "You're going to be fine in a day or two."

"Who won?" Christy asked.

"The campers won this year. They're pretty happy about it too."

"It's because of me, isn't it?" Christy said.

"No, don't think that. You did a great job. You gave it all you had. I'm proud of you."

Christy rested her pink hands under her chin on the pillow. "At least I don't have to serve tables tonight."

The dean smiled at her joke and said, "So that was your motive for sitting on the world's largest ant farm?"

"There must be easier ways," Christy said, feeling a little better.

"Actually, you've been working hard serving your campers all week, and I think you've done a terrific job. I'd love to have you as a counselor any time."

"I don't feel I accomplished anything spiritually with the girls. I tried talking to them about their relationship with God, and I even sat down with some of them one-on-one. Either they said they were already Christians, or they didn't want to give their hearts to the Lord, or they just didn't get it."

The dean's face took on another one of his understanding expressions. "Christy, you've done your part. You've told them how to receive eternal life. How much they understand is up to God. And how they respond is up to them, not you."

"But none of them responded. At all."

"You don't know what's going on in their hearts. We've planted lots of seeds in these kids this week. Some of them might sprout a week from now, some ten years from now. That's God's business."

"I just wish I could do more," Christy said with a sigh.

"You can. You can pray. Always pray. Actually, it looks to me as though you're in a pretty good position to pray for us during the rest of the evening."

Christy wished she could see her "infirmity" with as much of a spiritual reason as Dean Ferrill did. After he left she thought about how he might be right. She couldn't do anything else tonight. She couldn't serve tables at dinner or practice with the counselors for their closing-night skit. She couldn't even have her final night of devotions with her girls. The camp secretary was going to stay in Christy's cabin that night so she could remain in the infirmary. About the only thing she could do was pray.

Wiggling her still-stinging legs under the rough sheet, Christy tried to find a comfortable spot for her head on the pillow and began by praying for Jaeson and the other counselors. She prayed for her girls, all the other girl campers, and then all the boy campers. She prayed for the kitchen staff, office staff, leaders, and bus drivers. It didn't seem she had left out anyone except maybe herself.

She wasn't sure what to pray for herself. A quick recovery? For the sting to go away? Death to all red ants on planet Earth?

"Can she have visitors?" Christy heard Jaeson asking the nurse.

"Sure, go on in. She can't move, so why don't you take this stool. You can sit by the head of the cot."

Christy tried to twist her neck around without moving the rest of her body. She saw Jessica holding a plastic cup with wildflowers and Jaeson following her with the nurse's stool. "Hi," she greeted them, trying to sound cheerful, while fully aware of how silly she must look with pink polka dots all over her face and arms.

"You poor thing,' Jessica said, planting herself on the floor cross-legged and holding up the cup of flowers. "I wonder where I can put these so you can see them."

"Right there on the floor would be fine. Thanks, Jessica. They're pretty."

Just then, a chorus of boys' voices started to sing under the slightly opened window. "The ants go marching one by one, hurrah, hurrah. The ants go marching up Christy's legs, hurrah, hurrah."

"Hey!" Jaeson yelled, opening the window all the way and sticking his face out where they could see him. "You guys are in big trouble! I've got all your names. You're going to get it!"

The boys immediately scattered. Jessica pressed her lips together to try to keep from laughing.

Christy broke the silence with a ripple of laughter. "That was pretty clever of them," she said.

Jaeson and Jessica laughed with her.

"Are you feeling any better?" Jessica asked.

"A little, I guess. Sorry I won't be able to help you guys serve tables. And I'm really sorry I made us lose the race."

"Don't worry about it," Jaeson said. "I feel awful since I'm the one who showed you that hiding place. I promise there weren't any ants two years ago when I hid there."

"It's not your fault, Jaeson," Christy said. "I should have looked before I crawled in or at least worn jeans. I was going to take a towel, but I left it in the canoe. I feel bad because I'm letting you down with the dinner and the counselors' skit and everything."

"We were able to rework the skit. It's going to be fine. The main thing is that you get better, Christy."

"I'll try," she said.

"We need to get ready for dinner," Jessica said. "We'll check on you later, okay?"

"Oh, Jessica, if you have time, could you braid Sara's hair? I promised I'd do it for the dinner tonight."

"Sure. Anyone else you want me to check on for you? I think the camp secretary is already up in your cabin."

"No. Just tell them all I said hi, and I'll see them in the morning."

Jessica adjusted the cup of flowers on the floor so they faced Christy. "I think the purple ones are the prettiest," Jessica said. Then kissing the tip of her finger, she touched the "kiss" to the end of Christy's nose.

Christy smiled up at her and said, "That's about the only place on me that didn't get bit!"

Jaeson and Jessica left. She felt awfully alone.

"I'm going to dinner," the nurse announced about fifteen minutes later. "I'll bring something back for you. Are you too warm or too cold?"

"No, I'm fine. I'm getting a little stiff, though. Can I at least turn on my side?"

"It'd be better if you could wait. The majority of your bites are on the back of your legs, and I want them to remain exposed to the air."

"Okay," Christy sighed. "Are you sure you didn't find this remedy in the medieval book of tortures under 'How to Drive a Person Crazy'?"

"At least you still have your sense of humor," the nurse called over her shoulder as she left.

Yeah, my sense of humor and I are going to have a great time tonight.

Christy tried to pray again, going through and remembering everyone she could think of at camp. Near the end, right after she prayed for the bus driver, she dozed off and didn't wake up until she heard the door open.

The nurse must be here with my dinner. I'm not exactly hungry. I sure could use something to drink, though.

Soft music began to play behind her, and she twisted her head to see Jaeson, dressed in a crisp white shirt with a black bow tie, walking toward her. He had a white towel draped over his arm, and in both hands he balanced a tray decked with his Walkman, a can of 7Up with a straw sticking out of it, and a plate of chicken, mashed potatoes, and green beans.

"Dinner is served," he said in his best British butler voice. "I asked the nurse if I could bring this to you for her."

Christy should have felt delighted and honored by Jaeson's clever display of attention. Instead, she felt helpless, lying there with her painted clown face, not even able to cut her own meat.

"You didn't have to do this," she said.

"Oh, yes I did. It's the camp rules. If one counselor causes another counselor to end up in the infirmary, said counselor must serve the invalid dinner."

"I'm not exactly an invalid," Christy said.

"Oh, really? Then you'll just have to pretend for me. Do you want a drink?" Jaeson sat on the stool, balancing the tray in his lap and cutting up Christy's chicken into little pieces. He seemed perfectly content to continue acting out his part.

That's when it hit Christy that everything with Jaeson that week *had* been pretend. The moonlight picnic, talking about their dreams, all his smiles at her on the archery field and at the pool. They were pretending to be boyfriend and girlfriend for the week.

Tomorrow she would leave, and Jaeson would start the game all over again with some other girl next week.

"Is that what all this is to you?" Christy asked. "One big game of pretend?"

"What do you mean?" Jaeson said, scooting closer to her cot and using his knees as a table for Christy to eat off of. He handed her the fork and smiled.

"I mean, I don't know anything about you, and yet you've treated me all week like I'm you're girlfriend."

Jaeson looked surprised. "Why? Because I taught you how to shoot an arrow and showed you the moon from a canoe?"

"I'm not accusing you of doing anything wrong," Christy said, realizing how unkind her statement must have sounded to a guy who was nice enough to bring her dinner. "I've been playing along the whole time. I've liked doing things with you and holding hands and the moonlight picnic and everything. It's just that tomorrow it's going to be all over, and it'll seem like it was just a dream."

"That's how it is," Jaeson agreed. "You'd better start on the potatoes. They're going to be cold soon."

Christy took a fork full of potatoes and regretted the way she had blurted out her thoughts.

"Dreams aren't bad, are they?" Jaeson said cautiously. "If you both know you're playing the same game, then it's okay, and nobody gets hurt, right?"

Christy thought that somehow it didn't seem right or feel right. She didn't know how to say it in a way that would make sense to Jaeson, so she took a bite of chicken and said, "This is good. Thanks for bringing it to me. I guess I was hungrier than I thought."

"You're very welcome. And if you're upset about anything I

said or did this week, I'm sorry. I wasn't trying to hurt you. I just wanted to enjoy the week with you.''

After Jaeson left, Christy lay alone in the quiet room thinking about his words. Why should they bother her? She had played the camp-romance game. She had wanted to. Why did her heart feel achy now?

It must be that I'm leaving tomorrow, and this whole dream will disappear. What will I have left of my relationship with Jaeson? He hasn't indicated he would ever want to see me again or that he would write or call. Take me out of the week and put in another girl, and I'll bet he would do everything the same with her. Next week he probably will.

Christy decided she and Jaeson had had a dream relationship. It had started in her head, and she had convinced her heart it was real. Tomorrow it would be gone, evaporated like a morning mist. And she already knew it would not be her head that would be sad, but her heart. This dream relationship would leave her craving more.

She had plenty of time to contemplate all this while she lay on her full stomach, listening to the sounds of the evening meeting floating through her window. From the roar of the campers' laughter, the counselors' skit must have been hilarious. The singing sounded good. Much better than it did when she sat in the middle of her girls and heard their high voices singing as loud as they could. From her position across the camp, the distant music sounded sweet. She hummed along softly when she recognized the songs they were singing and realized for the first time that every song they had learned that week was Scripture put to music.

What a great idea! Without knowing it, the kids have learned a dozen Bible verses this week.

The last song they sang was Christy's favorite. She had heard it for the first time more than a month ago at the God-Lovers Bible study. From her cot she softly sang along.

> *Eyes have not seen. Ears have not heard.*
> *Neither has it entered into the heart of man*
> *The things God has planned*
> *For those who love Him.*

Christy thought about her dreams, her fantasies, and her wishes. If the words to the song were true, which they had to be because they were from the Bible, then her dreams for her life were nothing compared to God's dreams for her. Her part was to love God. And that was a true dream relationship that started in her heart and went to her head. Why was it she kept having to relearn this same lesson?

Drifting off into a peaceful sleep, Christy dozed for some time before being awakened by the disturbing awareness that someone else was in the room, watching her.

She snapped her head up and squinted, looking around in the dark room. "Who's there?"

"It's me. Sara," the tiny voice came from behind her.

"What's wrong, Sara? Are you okay?" Christy asked, trying to wake herself up and remember why she was here and who Sara was.

Suddenly the light snapped on, and Sara stepped over to the stool and plopped herself down, ready to talk.

"I'm glad you're awake," Sara said. "Everyone else is at the campfire, but I had to talk to you."

Christy slowly opened her eyes, hoping they would adjust soon to the light. "Does anyone know you're here?"

"I asked Jessica, and she said it was okay. She fixed my hair for me tonight for the dinner. Do you like it?"

Christy peered at the pesky little "Skipper" doll. Jessica had made two thin braids on each side of Sara's hair and tied them together in back with a thin, pink ribbon. It looked like a fallen halo, and the rest of Sara's wild, blond hair billowed out beneath it.

"It's darling," Christy said. "What did you want to talk about?"

"Well, you know," Sara said shyly.

Christy remembered her promise from the night before to talk to Sara about what it was like to kiss a boy. She let out a deep breath. To think this little "angel" woke her up to ask about kissing was more than Christy had patience for at the moment.

"Sara, I don't know if this is such a good time."

Sara lowered her brown eyes and looked disappointed.

"I mean, isn't there someone else you could talk to after the campfire? Jessica, maybe?"

"I guess," Sara said slowly. She stood up, shuffling her feet and stalling by the door. "It's just that you said if we ever wanted to talk about giving our hearts to Jesus, that you would be happy to talk to us."

"Sara," Christy cried out, "don't leave! Come back here and sit down."

Sara plopped back down on the stool, looking surprised.

"I'm sorry," Christy said. "Of course I want to talk to you about Jesus. I thought you were here to talk about kissing."

"Oh, no," Sara said, the sparkle returning to her eyes. "I already asked Jeanine. She kissed Nick today in the woods during the counselor hunt, and she said it was kind of yucky. She only kissed him on the cheek when he wasn't looking, but she said it tasted like salty mud." Sara gave a little shiver. "I don't think I want to kiss a boy for a while."

"Good," Christy said, laughing. "It's better to wait until the boy is old enough to see the benefit of bathing more than once a month. It's also a whole lot better when it's the boy's idea too and not just yours. That will take a few years, though. Be patient."

"Don't worry, I will," Sara said.

"You wanted to ask me about how to become a Christian?" Christy prodded.

"Yeah. How do you do it?"

Christy was about to launch into a detailed explanation of how our sin separates us from God, how Christ is the sacrifice that paid our debt, that salvation comes from repenting of our sins and trusting our lives to Christ. But then a little voice in her head reminded her that the campers had been hearing that all week from the speaker. Sara wasn't asking *why* she needed to give her heart to the Lord; she was asking *how*.

"God already knows what you're thinking, Sara. Do you want to ask Jesus to forgive your sins and come into your heart?"

"Yes."

"Then tell Him."

"Isn't there a special prayer, or something I'm supposed to do?" Sara asked.

"No, this is between you and God. You be honest and tell Him you're sorry for all the things you've done that made Him sad. Then tell Him you want Him to rule your life."

"That's it?"

"Yes," Christy said, "because, you see, it isn't your words, it's what's in your heart that God looks at."

Sara started to cry. "That's what I want. I want God in my heart."

"Then let's pray, and you tell Him." Christy reached her stiff arm over to Sara and held her hand.

As she listened, Sara told God she was sorry. She asked Him to forgive her and come into her heart and ended with a hasty "Amen."

Looking up at Christy with tears sparkling in her eyes, Sara said, "I don't feel anything."

"I didn't either when I gave my heart to Jesus. But it's not a feeling. It's a promise. God will keep His part of the promise and forgive you. Now you have lots of years ahead to keep your part of the promise and fall in love with Him."

"I think I do feel different now," Sara said. "I feel good that I finally did it. I've been wanting to ever since that night in the cabin when you talked about this."

Christy looked into Sara's innocent face. She felt a ball of joy catch in her throat as she said, "You know what, Sara? The Bible says that all the angels in heaven are rejoicing right now because you've just joined God's family."

"Really?"

"Really!"

"I didn't know I meant that much to God."

"Oh, Sara," Christy said, feeling a tear of joy escape and skip down her cheek. "If you only knew! If you only knew!"

CHAPTER ELEVEN

Seventeen

"So who was the letter from today?" Katie asked Christy as the two of them were driving in Katie's car a few weeks later.

"Sara," Christy answered. "I found a card with the meaning of her name on it and sent it a few days after camp. Sara means 'Princess.' She said in her letter she put the card on the wall above her bed."

Christy glanced at Katie and could tell by the way her jaw was twitching that she was clenching her teeth. Whenever Katie held something inside, her cheek would ripple in tiny spasms.

"Is it still hard on you that I got to go to camp and you didn't?" Christy asked cautiously.

The last time she had brought up the subject, Katie had cried.

"It's getting better. I'm glad all your campers are writing to you. Sounds like they really love you a lot," Katie said. "I hope someday my turn will come to be a camp counselor. I know it sounds crazy, but that's a major goal for me."

"It doesn't sound like a crazy goal, Katie. Maybe next year. I can't help but think God will honor your heart's desire. Especially since you honored Him by abiding by your parents' wishes this year."

Katie shook her head and changed lanes as they neared Newport Beach. "Now Christy, you know God doesn't work in such predictable patterns. But doesn't it seem ridiculous the way my parents see things? I mean, here we are, driving alone in my car an hour and a half to Newport Beach to stay for the weekend, and they didn't even ask where I was staying, for a phone number, or anything. Yet when I wanted to go to camp, they said 'no' simply because it was associated with the church. They said they didn't want me to get too involved with religious people. Why are they like that?"

"Maybe they've seen too many weird things that have been labeled a church-thing even though Christianity had nothing to do with it," Christy suggested. "Think of all the horrible stuff on the news, and then they show some murderer who says God told him to do it. I think a lot of people have the wrong idea of what a true Christian is."

"I guess you're right. Now I understand why Doug said they named their group the 'God-Lovers.' "

"I think you're right," Christy said. "I heard him say once that his main goal in life is to love God. That must be how he came up with the name. By the way, let's be sure to call him right when we get to my aunt and uncle's to tell him we'll be there all weekend. I told Todd we were coming, but I don't know if he told Doug."

"I told Doug," Katie said.

"You did? When?"

"Oh, last week sometime. I just happened to be talking to him. What time is it?"

"You didn't tell me," Christy said, her curiosity aroused. "Did you call him, or did he call you?"

"Does it matter?"

"Maybe."

"Okay, I called him. There's no law against calling a guy, is there? Do you know what time it is?"

Christy checked her watch and smiled at her defensive friend. "It's 1:15, and no, there's not a thing wrong with it. I kind of like the idea of you and Doug together."

"Really?"

"He's a great guy, and I think you two make a cute couple."

"Now that I'm over Rick," Katie added. "Which, I might say, didn't take very long."

A smile crept onto Christy's face. She kept her thoughts to herself, but soon realized her best friend could read her mind anyway.

"I know what you're thinking," Katie said. "And you're right. Rick was one of those phases we all have to go through while we're growing up. Now that I have that out of the way, I'm ready for a real relationship."

"With someone by the name of Doug, perhaps?"

"Perhaps."

"You have my blessing on that one," Christy said. "So our plan is to get there, call Doug and Todd, and set up something for the four of us to do tonight."

Now it was Katie's turn to smile and keep her thoughts to herself. Only this time Christy couldn't read her best friend's mind. Katie kept a shadow of a smile on her face all the way to Uncle Bob and Aunt Marti's. But she began to act jittery when they arrived.

"We'll get our stuff out of the trunk later," Katie stated, looking down the street as they shut the car doors and started up the walk to Bob and Marti's luxurious beachfront house.

"What are you looking for?" Christy asked.

"Who, me? Nothing." Katie laughed when she said it. A nervous laugh that made Christy think maybe Katie was hoping to see Doug's truck already there.

"I'll ring the doorbell," Katie said, skipping a few steps ahead of Christy and pressing the doorbell three times. She looked over her shoulder again and smiled at Christy.

No one came to the door.

"We could just walk in," Christy suggested. "This *is* my aunt and uncle's house, you know. Come on."

"No, wait," Katie said, grabbing her arm. "I'd feel better if we waited for them to answer the door."

Again Katie pressed the buzzer. Ring, ring, ring. It was as if she were trying to signal in some kind of secret code.

Christy heard the rush of feet running up behind her. Before she could turn around, someone covered her head with a pillowcase and grabbed her hands behind her back.

She screamed and kicked her left foot into the blackness. "What's going on, Katie?"

"You're coming with us," a deep, gruff voice behind her said.

She could tell by the grip that a guy held her hands. Her heart was pounding from the surprise of it all, but she wasn't really afraid. This kidnapping had all the marks of something Katie had cooked up.

The guy led her down the front steps and what seemed to be over toward Bob's garage. She heard the garage door open and a truck engine start up. Katie was whispering something about "in the back."

Next thing Christy knew, she was being hoisted into the back of what she imagined to be Doug's truck, with the mysterious guy next to her holding her hands to keep her from removing the pillowcase. The truck backed out of the driveway with a bump and sped down the street at what seemed to be an alarming speed.

"Where are we going?"

"You'll find out," the gruff voice said.

The truck turned a corner so quickly, Christy thought she might fall over. Then came another quick turn and another. She had no idea where they were. Another fast turn caused her to lean against her captor. Before she could balance herself back to a sitting position, they flew over another bump and came to an abrupt halt.

"Get out," the voice ordered.

For the first time, she felt frightened. She had been so sure the kidnapping was something Katie had arranged for her birthday, which was in two days. But she was all turned around and had no idea where she was. She felt panicky.

The guy practically lifted her out of the back of the truck. Christy could feel another hand on her upper arm, helping her down.

"Okay, you guys," she said with a nervous laugh. "This is all real funny." She tried in vain to peer through the weave on the pillowcase.

Her escort led her in a circle on what felt like asphalt beneath her feet. Then he directed her to take one step up, then one step down, then a few steps to the right. Christy could hear the ocean, so she knew they couldn't be far from her aunt and uncle's house. But where? Who was holding her hands and directing her to walk forward with baby steps? It didn't feel like Todd. Doug, maybe? But then who was driving the truck?

They went a few more steps, and Christy thought she smelled her uncle's after-shave. "Uncle Bob, I can smell you," she blurted out.

Christy heard Katie's squelched giggle, but no one else made a sound. At first she thought it was just her guide and Katie. Now it seemed more people were around her, watching her, trying to muffle their footsteps. How many more? And where was she?

"This way," the gruff voice directed, urging her to the right. "Up two steps."

She knew her feet were now on cement. She felt a strong ocean breeze, and she could hear the roar of the waves. Christy was certain more people were around her. She could hear whispers and feet shuffling. Through the dense pillowcase she thought she smelled the scent of matches.

Another step forward, and she felt something light and buoyant brush across the left side of her head. It was a strange sensation. A strong urge came to bat at it, but her hands were still held firmly. Christy managed to catch a peek of gray cement at her feet when she looked down through the opening of the pillowcase.

Where am I?

With an unexpected yank, the pillowcase came off her head, her hands were released, and a loud blast of "Surprise!" nearly knocked her off her feet.

A crowd of all her beach friends stood before her on Uncle Bob and Aunt Marti's wildly decorated patio, singing "Happy Birthday" and beaming over their big surprise.

Todd held out a huge birthday cake. It was loaded with pink frosting roses and seventeen lit candles. Todd's silver-blue eyes met hers as the song ended.

With a smile he said, "Go ahead, Kilikina. Make a wish."

Catching her breath, Christy stared at the cake. A tiny little runner in her brain took off sprinting for her "wish" file and pulled out the first thing it found there. Then the runner dashed back from the file to present her with her wish.

I wish I could go to Europe, she thought, and she blew out the candles with one big puff.

Everyone clapped. Todd set the cake down on the patio table, where Aunt Marti set to work cutting slices and invited the guests to scoop their choice of ice cream.

Christy laughed with her friends as they chattered about how shocked she looked when they took off the pillowcase.

"I want to know who put that thing on my head," Christy said.

"Me," Doug admitted. "You and Katie came too early, and your aunt told us to think of some way to stall you."

"We had to drive you around the block," Bob added. "Hope you weren't too shaken by the experience."

"I figured it was you guys, of course," Christy said, looking at Doug. "But I couldn't imagine what was going on or where we were."

"Your uncle drove my truck," Doug said. "Can't say he's the smoothest person I've ever met when it comes to shifting gears."

Katie handed Christy a huge piece of cake with a mound of chocolate chip ice cream smashed into the pink rose on top. "Did we surprise you?"

"Slightly! When did you plan all this?"

"Your aunt called me last week, and we put our heads together. That's why I acted so casual when you invited me to come here for the weekend. I kept the secret pretty well, don't you think?"

"No kidding! I had no idea. Thanks, Katie. I was definitely surprised."

"That's for later," Katie said, pointing up.

Christy looked up at the pink pig piñata strung from the slatted wood covering over the patio. She noticed the whole patio was laced in crepe-paper streamers and dozens of bright-colored balloons. It kind of looked as though a five-year-old was having a party, but she liked it. She knew her aunt had thrown herself into making the party a success.

All of Christy's beach friends were there: Heather, Tracy, Brian, Leslie, Doug, Todd, and a few others. But Christy glanced around and noticed Rick wasn't anywhere in sight.

"Everyone," Marti called out, waving her hands above her head to get their attention. Being petite was not an advantage to her at this moment. Her best advantage was that she had managed to keep a youthful flair about herself.

"As soon as you're finished with your cake and ice cream, there's a trash can over in the corner. The ice chests in both corners are filled with cold drinks anytime you want one this afternoon. Bob and Todd are going to set up the volleyball net, aren't you, boys?"

Bob gave Marti a playful salute. "One volleyball net coming up."

"We'll open gifts after the barbecue tonight," Marti continued. "And this sliding door will be open all afternoon, if you need to come in to change or anything. Now all of you have fun on the beach and remember to use your sunscreen."

"I'll get our stuff out of the car," Katie told Christy. "Are you still surprised?"

"I think I'll be in shock for the rest of the day!"

Katie smiled and said, "Good." As she turned to go, her copper-colored hair swished like an oriental fan whispering open.

Christy couldn't finish her humongous piece of cake and asked Todd if he wanted the rest of it. He held up his hand and shook his head.

"Try Doug," he suggested. "He has a higher tolerance for

pink sugar roses than I do."

"Todd," Bob called out from the sand a few yards away, "are you going to help me with this?"

"Sure," Todd called back. Then giving Christy a squeeze on the elbow, he said, "See you on the beach."

It took Christy and Katie only ten minutes to change into their bathing suits and cover-ups in the guest room and scamper down the stairs to join the group.

As they stepped out onto the sand, Christy said, "I notice Rick isn't here."

"Is that a problem?" Katie said.

"I don't know, is it?"

Katie stopped, her feet burrowing down in search of cooler sand. "What is that supposed to mean?"

"Did you not invite Rick because of how things turned out between you two? I mean, he's close friends with Doug and Todd. He's going to hear about the party."

"I asked Doug to call him," Katie explained. "I didn't want to talk to him. He told Doug he might show up later in the day. We planned this to be a day-long party, in case you hadn't figured that out. Your aunt is the ultimate party woman. She bought steaks for everyone for the barbecue and stuff for s'mores around the campfire. She rented a stack of movies in case anyone wants to stay up for a marathon movie night. I'm not going to hold my breath, but Rick might show up later. If he does, I promise to be civil to him."

"Okay, that makes me feel better. As long as you invited him, that's the main thing. What he does with the invitation is his choice. I just don't want him to feel shut out."

"Don't worry. I may not cherish the thought that I once was somewhat interested in Rick—," Katie said.

Christy interrupted with a roll of her eyes at Katie's understatement.

"But I have a good teacher showing me how to be friends with a guy after the crush is over."

"Who, me?" Christy said.

"No, the Little Mermaid," Katie teased. "Of course you."

Christy thought back to what a great teacher Jessica had been to her at camp, and she said, "You know, I think once we figure out what real love is, it becomes clear we can never love a person too much."

Katie looked thoughtful. Then tilting her head, she looked at Christy and said, "Is this what happens when you're about to turn seventeen? Your mind fills with deep ponderings, and you can suddenly explain the meaning of life to the rest of the world?"

Before Christy could answer, a bright orange volleyball flew through the air, bopping Katie on the top of her head.

"Hey!" Katie called out, spinning around, scooping up the ball and looking to see who threw it.

"Over here!" Todd called. "You're on our team, Katie. You want to play, Christy?"

She hesitated. Christy had never been good at sports like Katie was. But this was her birthday party. She imagined a person should be able to overcome at least some of her self-consciousness by the time she turned seventeen.

"Sure," she hollered back at Todd. "Which team am I on?"

"I need you over here," Uncle Bob said.

For the next hour, an intense game of volleyball ensued. Christy had a lot of fun, even though she didn't get the ball over the net too many times. Doug, Bob, and two of the other girls on her team made up for Christy's less-than-stellar performance. In the end, Todd and Katie's team won.

Todd somehow came up with the idea that the winning team should throw its opponents into the ocean. Before Christy realized what was happening, Todd single-handedly wrestled her down to the shore with a little-boy grin plastered all over his face.

Christy screamed and wiggled, but Todd held her arm tight. Just when her feet touched the cool, foamy part of the wave at the shoreline, she thought she had a chance to make a break for it. That's when Doug rushed up behind them.

"Yahoo!" Doug screeched, wrapping his gorilla-length arms around both Todd and Christy and taking them with him on his kamikaze plunge into the wave.

The three friends came up for air, laughing, dripping, and splashing each other. Doug dove under the water and grabbed Christy's ankle. She pulled away and surprised Doug with a splash of water in his face when he surfaced. Another wave crashed on them, tumbling them all to the shore.

Christy stood in the wet sand, still laughing and wringing the salt water from her oversized T-shirt, which now clung to her.

"Ready for another dip?" Doug asked.

"Maybe after I get the sand out of my ears," Christy said. "But I noticed Katie looking awfully relaxed over there." She pointed to Katie, who was lying stomach-down on her beach towel.

"Say no more," Doug said.

He and Todd charged through the sand, startling Katie from her rest. Within minutes they had pulled their three-point plunge maneuver into the ocean.

Christy retreated to Katie's now-vacant towel next to Tracy and Heather and tried to dry off.

I guess some things never change, she thought, remembering summers past on this same beach when she and these girls had watched Todd and Doug perfect their "throw the screaming girl into the ocean" routine.

Christy stretched out her long legs on the towel and felt the hot July sun drying up all the salty beads on her legs. Planting the palms of her hands behind her in the sand, Christy gazed out at the shimmering blue ocean. Katie's red hair popped up from under a wave. Next came Doug with his contagious laugh dancing toward her on the ocean breeze.

Todd, like a playful dolphin, rode the next wave to the shore. Then emerging from the water, he tilted his head back and shook his sun-bleached blonde hair so that all the droplets raced down his back. Christy had watched Todd shake his hair that way many times, but this was the first time she noticed what a distinct Todd-thing it was.

I'm glad some things don't change. I wish I could be this age, on the beach, with these friends, for the next fifty years. I don't want things to change. Ever.

Christy realized she was wishing almost the opposite of everything she had wished before. For years she had wished things would be different, especially that her relationship with Todd would change and move forward. Now she wanted it all to stop and stand still so she could observe and enjoy every little pinch of her life.

She knew the empty feeling when a camp romance ends. She knew the heady pleasure of dating a guy like Rick. And she knew the exquisite treasure of Todd's forever friendship.

Christy tilted her head back and felt the sun kissing her face and neck. She remembered Todd's blessing that she had passed on to Jeanine: "May the Lord make His face to shine upon you and give you His peace."

At this moment, Christy knew His forever peace. She felt His face shining upon her. With her eyes closed and a smile tiptoeing onto her lips, Christy silently made seventeen wishes. And all of them started with Todd.

Don't Miss These Captivating Stories in
THE CHRISTY MILLER SERIES

FOCUS ON THE FAMILY®
LIKE THIS BOOK?